THE CLUE OF
The Velvet Mask

Books by

CAROLYN KEENE

Nancy Drew Mystery Stories

Dana Girls Mystery Stories

The girls were suddenly awakened to their danger

NANCY DREW MYSTERY STORIES

THE CLUE OF
The Velvet Mask

BY CAROLYN KEENE

NEW YORK

Grosset & Dunlap

PUBLISHERS

Contents

THE CLUE OF
The Velvet Mask

CHAPTER I

A Suspicious Masquerader

"You look lovely, Nancy, and very mysterious," said Hannah Gruen, housekeeper for the Drew family, as she smiled fondly at the slender, blue-eyed girl.

Nancy had just finished dressing for a masquerade party, which she was attending with Ned Nickerson. Costumed as a Spanish señorita, she wore a red gown with a long sweeping skirt and a black lace mantilla.

Peering at herself in the full-length mirror, Nancy straightened a black wig which covered her naturally wavy, golden hair. Her friendly blue eyes peered mischievously above a fetching black lace mask.

"Thank you, Hannah," she remarked, and added gaily, "that's just the way I feel—almost as if something exciting might happen at the party tonight!"

1

"Oh, no!" exclaimed the housekeeper. Sighing, she added, "But I know those hunches of yours."

At this moment tall, handsome Carson Drew, Nancy's father, walked into the living room and sat down in his favorite chair. "You look very bewitching," he said. "But don't let some black-eyed villain creep into the evening."

Nancy laughed. "I make no promises."

Actually, Mr. Drew was very proud of the many baffling mysteries Nancy had solved. He was proud, too, of her quick mind and striking beauty. Never had she appeared more lovely than on this June night as she stood in the lamp's glow, gazing mischievously at him over her huge black fan.

"There'll never be too many mysteries for me," Nancy declared. Dropping the fan into her father's lap, she put on a pair of gold hoop earrings.

"Ah! Now you're really a siren," Mr. Drew joked. "By the way, where is Ned?"

Ned Nickerson was a college student, who dated her now and then.

"He'd better get here soon or you'll both be late."

It was now eight thirty. Ned was to have called at eight o'clock to don a costume Nancy had rented for him from the Lightner Entertainment Company.

The masquerade party was to be held at the Hendrick estate. Gloria Hendrick had been one of Nancy's school friends and had requested that everyone come early.

As Nancy glanced anxiously at the clock, the doorbell rang. "There he is now!" she exclaimed.

Nancy ran to open the door, and greeted the good-looking college football player with a sweeping curtsy.

"Wow!" he exclaimed with a quick intake of breath. "You're dynamite, Nancy! What a getup! And I'm sorry to be late. I had to drive Dad and Mother to the theater. Wish they could have seen you first, though."

"Never mind the compliments." Nancy laughed, pulling Ned into the living room. "I have a costume for you. Please put it on quickly."

"Not so fast! Do I have to go in fancy clothes?"

"You'll like the outfit. Linda Seeley selected it personally."

"Who's Linda?" Ned demanded suspiciously.

"We used to go to school together. She now works at the Lightner Entertainment Company."

Nancy produced a large cardboard box. Opening it ceremoniously, she spread out an eighteenth-century Spanish grandee's costume.

"Isn't it handsome, Ned? A plumed hat and high-heeled boots! A white neck ruff, too, and lace cuffs!"

Ned gave an indignant snort. "You expect me to wear that?"

"You'll make such a distinguished-looking Spanish grandee," Nancy coaxed. "Please, Ned."

"Oh, all right, since you're such a pretty Spanish lady," Ned acquiesced with a grin. "Those trousers look skimpy, though."

"I'll help pour you into them," Mr. Drew offered.

The two retired to an upstairs bedroom. During the next ten minutes weird sounds filtered down to Nancy and Mrs. Gruen. They were certain that the costume would be ripped to shreds before Ned's muscular body could be encased in it.

But presently he appeared on the stairway landing. Assuming a theatrical pose, he asked, "How do I look, Nancy?"

"Oh, wonderful! The costume fits perfectly."

Self-conscious, Ned came down the stairs to help Nancy with her cloak. Mr. Drew walked with them to Ned's car which was parked in front of the house.

"If Nancy makes you help solve a mystery, Ned, be careful of those rented clothes," the lawyer said jokingly.

Ned promised, saying he hoped something exciting would turn up.

"It may at that," Mr. Drew replied. "Keep your eyes open at the party."

Nancy glanced quickly at her father. "Why, Dad, you sound as if you thought something might go wrong! Have you some information you're keeping to yourself?"

"Possibly."

"Then tell us! Why all the mystery?"

"If you've been reading the papers, you know that one or more clever thieves have been attending parties given by wealthy people living around River Heights. Thousands of dollars in gems and other valuables have been stolen from their homes."

"You think he may show up at Gloria's party?" Nancy gasped.

"Well, it would be a likely place. I have no direct tip, Nancy. I'm merely advising you and Ned to be on the alert."

Nancy was intrigued. "Who knows?" she mused. "We may even capture this thief if he should be present this evening."

"The leader is an unusually smooth crook," the lawyer went on. "He's been eluding the police for months."

Nancy would have plied her father with further questions if it had not been so late. Assuring him that they would be on the lookout for any trouble-makers, she and Ned drove directly to the Hendricks' home.

The gala affair was in full swing when they arrived. Dancers filled the ballroom which blazed with light from the crystal chandeliers overhead.

"I don't recognize anyone," Nancy declared as they watched the masqueraders.

A short-skirted ballerina and her escort in a minstrel suit danced near by, doing intricate Charleston steps. Pierrot and Pierette sailed past, then a wooden soldier and china doll. Among the more unusual characters were Harlequin and Punchinello, the latter with a realistically humped back.

Presently Ned and Nancy were recognized by two of their closest friends. Bess Marvin, a plump, jolly girl, was dressed as a southern belle. Another girl, George Fayne, who was her cousin, rushed over to greet them. With her short haircut and slim figure, George could fool anyone in her disguise as a boy.

"Hi!" she exclaimed enthusiastically. "It's a wonderful party, but the dance floor is packed."

"Any villains here?" Nancy asked, and told her friends of her father's warning.

"Oh, how dreadful!" Bess exclaimed as her escort, Dave Evans, came up.

"If there are any villains here, they're masked," said George. "Just the right kind of night for a mystery, too."

"Oh, stop it," Bess begged, and offered to show Nancy and Ned where the checkrooms were. She and George led the way upstairs, together with

George's escort, Burt Eddleton, and Dave. After they had left their wraps, Nancy suggested pausing a moment in the second-floor library to look at the art treasures.

Although small, the room contained many rare paintings, antique vases, and a priceless collection of miniatures in a glass case. Some were solid-silver figurines, others portraits painted on porcelain. One of these, a likeness of Marie Antoinette, was especially attractive. Nancy noticed that the case was not locked.

"This is just making it easy for a thief," she remarked.

"Not so loud or you'll have a detective at our heels," Ned cautioned.

"I doubt that there's one in the place," George replied. "Gloria's parents never seem to worry about their valuables."

"Oh, let's forget about robberies," Bess pleaded. "This is supposed to be a gay party."

"Right-o," approved Ned, seizing Nancy's hand. "Let's dance."

For the next half hour the young people had a wonderful time. The music was superb and Nancy forgot everything but Ned's expert leading. After a samba which left her rather breathless, she saw Linda Seeley standing near the refreshment table. The girl was not in costume, and obviously had attended the party as an employee of the Lightner Entertainment Company.   Nancy took Ned over and both lifted their masks.

"Oh, hello, Nancy," Linda greeted her.   "Did you approve of the costumes I sent out?"

"Perfect.   The party's lovely, too."   Nancy introduced Ned.

"I'm glad you're enjoying it, because I planned the party—or rather my company did.   I wouldn't be here tonight except that my boss, Mr. Tombar, couldn't come at the last minute. I do so hope everything goes all right."

"Of course it will."

"The truth is, we didn't plan on so many people."

"Crashers?" Ned asked.

"I'm afraid so.   We warned the family to be careful about admitting only guests who could present invitations, but they didn't want anyone checked at the door."

As the night wore on, the ballroom became very warm.   Seeking the cool air outside, Nancy and Ned sat awhile on a garden bench. Then they decided to dance again.   As they arose, Nancy searched in vain for her mask.

"I must have dropped it somewhere on the path," she declared.

Quickly they retraced their steps.   The mask was nowhere in sight.   As they continued to look for it they heard footsteps on the shadowy, gravel path.

A tall man dressed in a flowing, black broad-cloth cloak appeared. As his back was turned to them, he did not notice the watching couple.

The man, who was unmasked, paused to examine a rose trellis which extended from the ground to the second story of the house. He put his left foot on it and reached up with his right arm.

"What's he up to?" Ned muttered.

The masquerader must have heard the question, for he stepped down quickly. Even then, Ned and Nancy did not see his face. Abruptly the man scooted down the path and hastened back to the house.

"Ned, do you suppose he intended to climb the trellis to the library?" Nancy asked.

"It would make a handy ladder." The young man strode over to inspect it.

At the base he picked up a black velvet hooded mask. Ned thought that the man in the black cloak might have dropped it.

"Since you can't find your mask, Nancy, try this one for size," he suggested.

Normally, Nancy would have done no such thing. But instinct told her that she might be on the trail of the mysterious party thief!

"I'll wear the hood until we see the man in the black cloak," she agreed.

Returning to the ballroom, she and Ned found the floor even more crowded. In vain, Nancy looked about for the mysterious stranger. Then, unexpectedly, he cut in on Ned!

But now he wore a mask exactly like the one Nancy had on! Before Ned could recover from his surprise, the stranger waltzed away with Nancy.

"I had a deuce of a time finding you in this crowd," he scolded irritably. "Why didn't you wear the Oriental costume you said you would? If it weren't for the mask, I never would have recognized you."

Nancy remained silent, but her heart was thumping. Someone in an Oriental costume must have dropped the mask Nancy was wearing.

"You nearly wrecked our plan, stupid!" the man went on. "Can't you ever learn to obey orders?"

The dancer in the black cloak now saw Ned coming to reclaim his partner.

"Here comes that pest again," he muttered. "Get rid of him as soon as you can."

A moment before Ned tapped him on the shoulder, the man thrust a note into Nancy's hand. She managed to hide her astonishment as they danced away, but once beyond the man's view, Nancy paused beside a cluster of palms. Tersely she explained to Ned what had happened.

"I'm sure that man is the party thief. He mistook me for someone else because of this hooded mask."

She unfolded the message which had been thrust into her hand and read it in an undertone.

" 'Eastport Trellis Company offers secondhand window sash on cash terms.   In case of rain every cloud has a silver lining.' "

"It must be a hoax, Nancy!"

"I don't think so," she replied soberly.   "No, Ned, this message is in code.   We must decipher it! The safety of the Hendricks—and everyone here —may depend on what we find out!"

CHAPTER II

A Daring Theft

NANCY and Ned reread the mysterious note several times, trying to figure out its meaning.

"There's a trellis company in River Heights," Ned declared thoughtfully. "It's not called the Eastport, though. And it doesn't sell window sash or any secondhand lumber."

"That's not it, I'm sure, Ned."

"Maybe the word *trellis* refers to the one in the garden."

"Yes, and the trellis is on the east side of the house."

"Sure! East trellis! But where do we go from there?"

"The man in the black cloak was looking up at the second-floor windows of the library, Ned. Does that suggest anything?"

"A robbery!"

"Right. If we can decipher this note, we may be able to stop it."

"The code's beyond me, Nancy."

"I don't believe it's actually in code. But if one drops out certain unessential words—"

"Say, I get it!" Ned broke in. " 'East trellis—second window—cash.' "

"The second window opens into the library," Nancy reminded him. "Probably it's unlocked. This note must mean that there's plenty of cash or valuables for any thief who climbs that trellis."

"How do you interpret the second sentence of the message? 'In case of rain every cloud has a silver lining.' "

"That has me puzzled unless—why, that must be it!"

"What, Nancy?"

"In case—silver. The silver miniatures in the glass case!"

"You've hit it!" Ned exclaimed. "I'll bet they intend to pull a job here tonight—at any minute!"

"We'll have to work fast to stop them. Ned, station yourself at the trellis and keep watch. I'll rush up to the library and see what's going on there."

"Better notify the police."

"Just as quickly as I can reach the library," Nancy assured him. "I noticed a telephone there—if the wires haven't already been cut."

The two separated. Nancy looked quickly

about the ballroom, hoping to see some of her friends, a member of the Hendrick family, or Linda Seeley. But every person who might have aided her seemed to have disappeared. Nancy ran swiftly up the circular stairway which led to the second floor.

The moment was a critical one. In the past, however, the girl detective frequently had been called upon to think fast in an emergency. Because of this unusual ability she was well known and respected in River Heights.

Adored by her many friends, Nancy also was admired for her ability to solve mysteries. Her first case, turned over to her by her father, had been called *The Secret of the Old Clock*. Since that time Nancy had helped countless persons and faced many dangers for them, her latest adventure being known as *The Mystery at the Ski Jump*.

Nancy's mother had died when the girl was very young. Since then, Mrs. Gruen had managed the Drew household. She loved Nancy as her own daughter and worried about the dangerous situations in which the young detective often found herself.

Now, intent only upon preventing a robbery at the Hendrick home, Nancy gave no thought to personal danger. She reached the first landing, beyond view of the ballroom. There she was stopped short. Confronting her was a feminine masquerader in a glittering Javanese costume.

Could she be the woman who was supposed to have worn a black velvet hooded mask? Now she had on a black lace face mask, probably the one that Nancy had lost.

For an instant the two stared at each other. Nancy caught a glimpse of dark, piercing eyes and a cruel mouth. Her observations went no further, for without warning the lights went out.

At that same instant the woman seized Nancy's wrists in a strong grasp and thrust a hand over the girl's mouth.

Nancy struggled frantically to free herself. With her hooded mask she was at a disadvantage. She was amazed at the strength of the woman masquerader. The two scuffled on the landing, while in the ballroom below there were calls and cries of alarm.

The woman tried to rip off the hooded mask, but instinct told Nancy to hold onto it. Then as suddenly as she had been seized, the girl was released. The woman in the Javanese costume raced down the stairs and disappeared in the darkness. Recovering her breath, Nancy removed the mask and groped her way up the staircase.

Suddenly the lights went on and Nancy hurried along the hall. Before she could reach the library, a maid came running from it.

"Help! Police!" she screamed. "The house has been robbed!"

Nancy stopped the frightened girl, advising her to be quiet and not start a panic on the crowded floor below.

"Quick!" she urged the maid. "Tell me what happened. Did a thief break into the library?"

"Y-yes. Fifteen minutes ago," the maid informed her. "Through the window. I had my back turned. Suddenly a hand was clapped over my mouth from behind. My hands were tied quick as a flash. Then a blindfold was slipped over my eyes, and I was gagged."

"How did you get them off?"

"I managed to free myself just as the lights went on. But everything's been taken except the wall paintings!"

"The silver miniatures too?"

"Yes, miss—all that could be carried off easily."

"Which way did the thief go? Down the stairway or out the window?"

"I couldn't say. He went as quietly as a cat."

"It was a man? Not a woman in a Javanese costume?"

"She was the lookout, I think. Before I was grabbed I saw her wandering around on the second floor."

From the maid's account, Nancy knew that the daring robbery had been well planned. Undoubtedly the masquerader who had seized her on the landing had been stationed there to see that the real thief made a successful getaway.

Shutting off the lights had served a good purpose. Under cover of darkness, the thieves had escaped!

Though convinced that it was already too late to capture any member of the bold gang, Nancy raced downstairs. Reaching the garden, she called Ned's name. His answering shout informed her that he still remained on guard at the trellis.

"What happened?" he demanded as she ran up. "I saw the lights go off."

"The house has been robbed!"

"Not the library?"

"Yes, and the thief must have escaped through the window."

"No one has come down the trellis since I've been here."

"Then either he got away before you went on guard or he slipped out of the house while the lights were off," Nancy declared, and then added, "What's this?"

She stared at a tiny piece of cloth which had snagged on a protruding nail in the trellis.

"It must have been torn from that man's cloak!" Nancy exclaimed as she removed it. "Ned, it's a good clue. Come on. Let's see if that man who danced with me is still around."

Re-entering the house, Nancy and Ned looked for him, but he was not among the guests who now had removed their masks. The couple learned that the police had been summoned by Linda Seeley. The girl was deeply distressed, fearful that the Hendrick family, despite her warning to them, might blame her for what had taken place.

"I was afraid that this very thing would happen!" she moaned. "If only a closer check had been made of the guests!"

Nancy and Ned instigated a search of both the house and grounds, but as they had expected, no trace was found of the woman in Javanese garb or the man in the black robe. An empty parking space near the entrance to the grounds indicated that they had probably left by automobile.

The scream of a siren announced the arrival of a police car. Detectives inspected the library, ascertaining that the thief had entered through the second-story window. From information provided by Nancy and the maid, it was deduced that the man had been aided by at least two others inside the house—probably the woman in the Javanese costume and someone who turned off the lights.

All guests were subjected to a thorough questioning. The officers listened attentively when Nancy and Ned told their story and showed the note, the piece of cloth, and the velvet mask.

"You're Miss Nancy Drew, the girl detective, aren't you?" asked one of them.

"Yes, Lieutenant Kelly," she replied.

"Well, we're certainly obliged to you for this evidence," he said, examining the articles. "You say that man you danced with had on a mask like this one?"

"Yes. And, Lieutenant Kelly, would you mind letting me take the mask home? I'd like to show it to my father. He said that I might run into one of the party thieves tonight. I'll bring the mask to headquarters any time you want it."

Kelly thought a moment. "I guess it's all right, Miss Drew. Maybe you'll figure out a clue from it," he complimented her. "I'll phone you when we need it."

In the meantime his assistant, Detective Ambrose, a brusque young policeman, had sought out Linda Seeley and was bringing her to the group.

"You're in charge of this party?" he was saying gruffly.

"Yes, officer," Linda replied meekly. "That is, I am in the absence of Mr. Tombar. At the last minute he had other business to attend to, so he asked me to substitute here for him."

The detective shot rapid-fire questions at the frightened girl. Who was Mr. Tombar? What company had arranged the party? What precautions had been taken to guard the valuables? Why hadn't invitations been checked more carefully?

Feeling that the detectives were trying to blame

her, Linda answered hesitantly. The questions became more pointed. Suddenly Ambrose said:

"You'd better come along to headquarters."

"You're accusing me?" Linda gasped. "On what grounds?"

"You'll find out. Just follow me," Ambrose ordered.

Bursting into tears, the girl ran to Nancy.

"Don't let them take me to jail," she pleaded, clinging to her friend.

Mrs. Hendrick moved forward. "Why, this is dreadful!" she said. "Do you have to arrest her, officer?"

"Sorry, but I must do it."

"I swear I had absolutely nothing to do with the robbery!" Linda cried out. "Oh, Nancy, you've got to help me!"

CHAPTER III

Conflicting Stories

NANCY knew that the detectives could not arrest Linda without evidence. How unjust to frighten her!

"Miss Seeley did not commit the robbery," she said. "Early in the evening she told me that she was worried because so many uninvited guests must have come. There were many more people here than were invited."

"Is this true, Mrs. Hendrick?" Detective Ambrose asked.

"I'm afraid it is," the hostess replied. "We were very foolish not to have taken Miss Seeley's advice and ask our guests to show their invitations."

By now, Ambrose had recognized Nancy as the daughter of Carson Drew.

"If you say this girl is all right, Miss Drew, I'll take your word for it," he said.

21

"Linda is a friend of mine."

"That's good enough for me," the officer replied.

"Come along, Linda," Nancy invited, taking her by the arm. "Ned and I will drive you home."

After they picked up their wraps, Gloria Hendrick walked with them to the front door. She smiled kindly at the distressed girl.

"We know it wasn't your fault, Linda," she said, "but we have suffered a dreadful loss and the party's ruined. Oh, Nancy, I wish you'd work on the case and help us get back our valuable miniatures. Will you?"

"I'll do what I can," Nancy answered. "But maybe the police will find the thieves."

On the way home Nancy had a sudden brain storm and asked Linda if anyone had rented a black cloak from her company.

"I don't think so, although several people at the party did rent costumes from us."

"And masks?"

"Yes, but not like the one you're carrying."

When Nancy reached home she found that her father had waited up for her. He was in his study, poring over some notes he planned to use the next day in court.

Sitting in the big leather chair beside his desk, Nancy related everything that had occurred at the party. Mr. Drew listened attentively, showing little surprise at the disclosure that a robbery had taken place.

"Here's the black velvet hood the police let me keep," Nancy concluded, handing the mask to her father. "I have a hunch it may be an important clue in the case."

"How well do you know Linda Seeley, Nancy?"

"Not too well," she admitted, troubled by the question. "We attended the same school."

"Your friend may find herself in serious trouble," the lawyer hinted. "For that matter, the Lightner Entertainment Company already is having difficulties. Keep this to yourself, Nancy, but Mr. Lightner, the owner, has appealed to me to defend his firm against several threatened lawsuits."

"Who is bringing them?"

"Former customers whose homes were robbed during or after parties arranged by the company. They are demanding that he settle for the losses not covered by insurance, but he insists he's not liable. They've given him a couple of weeks to decide."

"You'll defend the firm, Dad?"

"I probably will. Before I definitely commit myself, though, I'd like to do a bit of investigating on my own in connection with the company. The trouble is, I'll be tied up on an involved real-estate litigation. The case will take me out of town, too."

"How about appointing me your deputy?" Nancy proposed eagerly. "I'd love to delve into the mystery!"

"I suspected as much," her father chuckled. "All right, Nancy. While I'm away tomorrow, suppose, as your first assignment, you check up on both Mr. Lightner and Linda and find out what you can."

"I'll do that—first thing," Nancy promised.

The Lightner office was situated on a narrow downtown street of River Heights. Early the next morning Nancy located it, and on the pretext of returning the Spanish costumes asked to see Mr. Lightner personally.

He was a short, slightly built man of exceedingly nervous manner and speech.

"What can I do for you?" he inquired. "I trust you found your costumes satisfactory?"

"In every respect, Mr. Lightner. One of your employees, Linda Seeley, selected them."

"Linda is a very capable girl," Mr. Lightner remarked. "She hasn't been here many months, but she learns fast. And she has clever ideas."

Having delivered himself of this speech, the company president became silent.

Nancy glanced around the room. The office walls were decorated with an unusual collection of weird-looking masks.

One cylinder-shaped head covering particularly fascinated Nancy, for long horns had been affixed to it. To another a red feather plume had been attached.

"You're interested in masks?" Mr. Lightner asked.

"Yes. You have a fine collection here."

"One I've accumulated over the years," he told Nancy proudly. "See that Fire God mask on the east wall? I got it from a Zuñi Indian chief in New Mexico."

Mr. Lightner went on to explain that these were ceremonial masks used among the Indians.

"Sometimes they are constructed to imitate animals."

"You have a great many velvet masks, I suppose?" Nancy asked thoughtfully.

"Yes. Most of them are kept in the wardrobe room. Would you like to see them?"

"Very much."

Mr. Lightner pressed a buzzer, summoning an employee named John Dale to show Nancy through the wardrobe rooms.

"I wish I had time to take you around myself," the president said regretfully. "I could talk myself hoarse on the subject of masks."

To draw him out a little further, Nancy asked if any particular history were connected with the wearing of black velvet masks.

"Oh, yes," he replied. "Men first wore them during the reign of Louis XIV. In that period of terror and political intrigue it wasn't safe to appear on the street except in disguise. Black velvet hoods were worn especially with wide-sleeved dominoes or robes."

"Do you have some of these robes for rent?"

"Yes. John will show them to you. He'll explain more about their history too."

Warmed by Nancy's enthusiastic interest, John Dale escorted her through the wardrobe rooms.

"In early days," he said, "French and English ladies used a great deal of powder and rouge. Masks served as a protection against sun, wind, and dust. Often they were lined with fine silk. As a further protection, glass sometimes was fitted into the eye openings."

Nancy switched the subject to black dominoes, saying she had been at the Hendricks' masquerade and danced with a stranger who wore one.

"I've been wondering who he is," she said. "Did you happen to rent such a costume?"

"No, I didn't," John replied. "Everyone who came to me wanted something spectacular. Would you like to see our black cloaks? We have several kinds."

"Why, yes, I would," Nancy replied, trying to stifle her excitement. It was possible that someone else had rented the costume to the thief!

The young man showed her a rack of black cloaks, some with attached hoods, some without. He was closing the glass door of the case when Nancy's gaze fastened upon a particular robe.

"Wait!" she exclaimed. "May I see that garment a moment?"

The long black cloak, which hung in graceful folds, had a slight tear near the hem. Examining it closely, Nancy noted that a tiny piece of material was missing.

"Was this cloak returned here today?"

"I don't know," John replied. "You'll have to ask the intake clerk. Or Mr. Lightner."

What a stroke of luck! She had come upon the very garment she sought. Surely this cloak with the missing bit of cloth must have been worn by the masked man she and Ned had seen at the garden trellis.

If her luck continued, she would soon learn the name of the person who had rented the costume!

"I'll see Mr. Lightner," she told John Dale. "Wait here. I'll be back in a moment."

CHAPTER IV

An Irate Employer

THE "MOMENT" which Nancy had expected to be gone stretched into ten minutes. She could not find Mr. Lightner immediately, but finally she saw him on the street about to get into his car. He returned with her to the costume room.

John Dale was no longer there, but he came back shortly, saying that Mr. Tombar, the assistant manager, had asked him to go on an errand.

"Now let's see this cloak you say has a hole in it," Mr. Lightner said to Nancy. "The costume never should have been returned to the rack without being repaired."

Twice Nancy looked through the costumes, examining every black cloak. The telltale one was not there!

"Did you remove the one which I pointed out to you?" she asked John, seeing an empty hanger.

28

"Why, no," he answered. "It was here when I was called away."

"Then someone else has taken it. You saw the cloak yourself only a few minutes ago."

"Yes, I did," the man replied.

Mr. Lightner checked with his other employees by telephone to their desks, but all denied having seen or moved the garment.

Though Nancy said little, suspicion was crystallizing in her mind. She felt sure that someone in the entertainment firm was not telling the truth—someone who might even be working with the party thieves! She was certain that John Dale was not guilty.

Another daring idea popped into Nancy's mind. Maybe the thief had borrowed the robe, returned it, and was hiding, waiting for a chance to escape, when Nancy had shown up.

"So he went off with the cloak again," she thought. Aloud she said to Mr. Lightner, "Would you mind telling me who rented the cloak?"

"Not at all. Every garment has a number. The one that belongs on this empty hanger is 4579. Come with me and we'll look into the matter."

Records showed that the cloak, a velvet mask, and accessories had been rented two days earlier by a James Flobear, Route 1, Brandon.

"That's a small town about twenty miles from

here," he explained. "I don't happen to know this Mr. Flobear."

Mr. Lightner's next remark stunned Nancy. He said that Linda Seeley had handled the transaction. But Linda had said the night before that she had not rented the black robe!

Summoned by Mr. Lightner, the girl denied any knowledge of the cloak. "I didn't know that costume had been rented," she declared. "Someone else put my initials on the typed slip. He's trying to shift the blame to me because a thief wore it!" she cried hysterically.

"What!" Mr. Lightner exclaimed.

He was very upset by her accusation and summoned every employee in the place. They all came except Mr. Tombar, who was busy with a customer. All denied any knowledge of the entry for the torn cloak or what had become of it.

Mr. Lightner paced the floor. "This is bad— very bad for our business," he declared. "This firm is old and has a fine reputation."

To break the tension Nancy said that she would like to know how the costume had been returned. To this question none of the employees had an answer, either.

Deeply troubled over the whole incident, Nancy decided to make an attempt to track down James Flobear. A short time later she left the entertainment company and called at the post office. From the postmaster, who was an old friend of her father, she learned that no one by the name of Flobear lived in or near Brandon.

"Just as I suspected," Nancy said to herself. "Obviously a false name was given so there could be no follow-up. And whoever had charge of the transaction at Lightner's is afraid to say so."

Nancy's next call was at the police station, where she talked directly with Chief Denny. He thanked her for her assistance the evening before and listened attentively to her story of the morning's happenings.

"You always seem to pick up a clue a little ahead of us." The chief smiled. "I'll send a man over to Lightner's to check up on the cloak episode."

Nancy asked if the police had at any time suspected the entertainment company in connection with the party robberies.

"You're asking for inside information, Miss Drew," the officer said. "But I know you'll keep anything I tell you confidential."

"Of course."

"We did suspect the company at first and had everyone in it shadowed for two weeks, even Mr. Lightner himself. But we didn't find out a thing that was suspicious about any of them. No, I guess we'll have to hunt for our thieves somewhere else."

"Last night Detective Ambrose seemed very suspicious of Linda Seeley who works there," Nancy said.

"You've caught me again," the chief owned up. "We do have our eye on Miss Seeley. No direct evidence against her, you understand. But she may be getting something out of this on the side."

"What do you mean?"

"She may be accepting a percentage on each haul for supplying information that pays off. Miss Seeley may be working with the gang and also with servants in the homes where big parties are arranged by the Lightner Entertainment Company."

Nancy remained thoughtfully silent. She had not realized that a police net was closing in around Linda!

"The girl has a clean record," the captain resumed. "We never would have suspected her if we hadn't been tipped off by her employer."

"Not Mr. Lightner?" Nancy gasped.

"No, by his assistant, Peter Tombar. When we talked to him after a robbery at a party which he and Miss Seeley took care of, he suggested that the girl might bear watching."

"But why?"

"Well, because she was in charge of certain parties at which robberies took place," the chief answered.

Nancy left the police station more troubled

than ever over Linda's predicament. Was Peter Tombar's distrust of the girl warranted?

"I think I'll go and have a talk with him," she reflected.

It was nearing the noon hour by the time she reached the Lightner offices. Most of the employees had gone to lunch, but Mr. Tombar was there. A secretary directed Nancy to a rear room where the man was inspecting an Egyptian mask made of painted plaster.

Peter Tombar cast an unfriendly glance at Nancy. He was a rather stout man, dark-complexioned, with a hard, determined set to his jaw.

At once, Nancy felt on the defensive. She divined instantly that Mr. Tombar would not cooperate unless it suited his purpose to answer her questions. Lowering her voice and assuming a confidential manner, she said:

"Mr. Tombar, I'm here to check up on one of your employees—a girl named Linda Seeley."

A glint of satisfaction flickered in the man's dark eyes. Immediately he became less guarded.

"In trouble with the police, isn't she?" he demanded. "I told Mr. Lightner a week ago that girl would get the company in hot water."

"Tell me what you know about her," Nancy asked.

"She's flighty. Scatterbrained, I'd call her."

"You've caught her in mistakes?"

"Well, not exactly," Mr. Tombar admitted

reluctantly. "She's crafty. Twists like a pretzel when you try to pin her down."

"Then you actually haven't anything against her?"

"Say, what is this—a police court?" he growled. "A man has his own reasons for not liking hired help and he doesn't have to tell why!"

Nancy flushed.

"By the way, have you any theory concerning the recent party robberies?" she asked calmly.

"I have!" Mr. Tombar returned with emphasis. "And I guess you know the person I mean."

Nancy nodded. But instead of being convinced that Linda was guilty, she felt an even stronger urge to help the girl. Tombar plainly disliked her and intended to have her discharged if he could find the excuse.

Nancy left his office and walked across the street. Her dislike of the man was increasing and she wondered what motive he had for casting suspicion on Linda. There was more to the mystery than had come to the surface yet.

Passing a drugstore with a soda counter, Nancy went in for a sandwich. To her delight she noticed that Linda was there too. She slid onto a stool beside her.

After giving her order, she drew Linda into conversation. The girl seemed very despondent, and Nancy could guess the reason.

"It's Mr. Tombar," Linda confessed. "He lectured me again this morning."

"What about?"

"The robbery last night, and the missing black cloak."

"The cloak hasn't been found?"

"Not yet. Mr. Lightner is most annoyed. Oh, everyone's in a frightful mood."

As Nancy stirred her hot chocolate, she said, "Tell me about Mr. Tombar. What's he like?"

"Vinegar and acid. He's efficient, though. Mr. Lightner depends on him, but Mr. Tombar's a slave driver, always bawling out employees if they're a minute late."

"I suppose he's always on time himself?" Nancy asked.

"Oh, yes. But he makes up for it by taking a two-hour lunch period nearly every day. He waits until the others get back, then goes off alone. He never eats with the other men."

"Where does he eat?" Nancy asked.

"I don't know," Linda answered. "Maybe out of town. He always takes his car."

Two hours for lunch was a long time for a strict disciplinarian like Tombar! The information interested Nancy, who mulled over it as she ate her sandwich.

"I must go now," Linda said with an anxious glance at the wall clock. "See you later."

Left alone, Nancy finished her own lunch leisurely and paid the bill. As she left the drugstore, she chanced to look across the street toward the Lightner offices.

Peter Tombar was just coming out, a package in his hand. Nancy saw him walk briskly to a green sedan parked a short distance away. A wild thought came to her. Did he have the torn cloak with him?

She noted that not only the wheels but the fenders were heavily caked with mud. Evidently Mr. Tombar had driven recently on unpaved roads in the country. He might be going there now to dispose of the cloak!

Nancy wished fervently that she might follow him, but she had not driven her own car downtown that morning. What miserable luck! Just when she needed it most!

A taxicab with a *vacant* sign rounded the corner. Instantly Nancy hailed the driver and hopped in. "Follow that green car ahead!" she directed as Mr. Tombar pulled out.

"Friend of yours?" The taximan grinned.

"No, just the opposite," Nancy replied, blushing.

"Okay, lady. Here goes!"

Nancy's worry that Peter Tombar might have seen her action and would lead the taxi a merry chase proved to be true. At high speed he turned right at the first corner. By the time the taxi reached the intersection, the green sedan was far down the side street.

"That old boy's sure stepping on it," the taxi driver declared. "You want me to keep him in sight?"

"I certainly do."

"Then sit tight, miss. And keep an eye out for cops!"

CHAPTER V

An Interrupted Party

THE TOMBAR car raced through a red light, whirling around a corner so fast that the two outer wheels actually seemed to leave the pavement.

"That fellow's a lunatic!" Nancy's taxi driver muttered.

"Take it a little slower," the girl advised nervously. "Even if we lose him, it's not worth a smashup."

As she spoke, they heard the shrill scream of brakes ahead. At the busy Cherry Street and White Avenue intersection, Tombar had sped through another red light. Oncoming traffic had halted barely in time to prevent a head-on collision.

Unmindful of the near accident, Tombar raced on. Nancy saw his car turn left at the first side street.

The taxi was forced to wait for the traffic light to change. When it finally reached the side street, the green sedan had vanished completely.

"Never mind. It's no use trying to pick up the trail now," Nancy told the driver after they had cruised around two blocks without seeing Tombar again. "He knew we were following him."

"He sure tried hard to shake us," the taximan agreed.

Nancy tipped the driver well for the brief but speedy ride. As she walked away, Peter Tombar's behavior convinced her that he did not want her to know where he was going. She decided his movements would bear watching.

The following day Nancy was waiting for Linda when she finished work. She offered the girl a ride home, and during the drive asked her if she knew what Mr. Tombar had in the package he had taken away the previous noon. Linda said she had no idea but that he was always carrying packages of one sort or another.

"In connection with his work?" Nancy questioned quickly.

"I imagine so," was Linda's vague response. Nancy questioned her on any big affairs the Lightner Entertainment Company had scheduled.

"Two luncheons tomorrow," Linda told her. "A small dinner party Monday—nothing fancy. Our business has fallen off a lot lately since the robberies have received so much publicity."

"Aren't there any big parties on the calendar?"

"Only the Becker wedding. Our company is making arrangements for that."

"When is the wedding, Linda?"

"Tuesday night, at their home."

"The Beckers are socially prominent people," Nancy said, thinking aloud. "There will be scads of expensive wedding presents. Just the sort of setup to tempt a thief."

"Don't suggest such a thing," Linda replied with a shiver. "It gives me cold chills to think of it. One more robbery and our company will be ruined."

"Then why not take special precautions?"

"Oh, we have! Mr. Tombar has arranged for plain-clothes men to watch the guests. As an added safety measure, Mr. Lightner himself suggested that a reliable servant be assigned to guard the wedding silver. Mr. Tombar thought that was entirely unnecessary, but he was overruled."

"Even so, there could be a slip-up," Nancy mused. "Those thieves are clever."

"How well I know! Oh, Nancy, I wish you were going to be there! You caught a glimpse of the thieves at Gloria's party and might recognize them if they dared appear again."

"Now that's an idea," Nancy agreed, quickly seizing upon the suggestion. "Can you get me an invitation?"

"Well—" Linda hesitated, then said decisively,

"yes, I can. I'll tell the Beckers that you're a Lightner Entertainment Company assistant."

"Which will be true," Nancy chuckled.

"If you prevent a robbery," said Linda, "you'll be the best little assistant the firm ever had! But if Mr. Tombar catches me doing this, he'll fire me for sure," she added uneasily. "You'll be very careful, won't you, Nancy?"

"Trust me. I shan't give you away. Just arrange it so that I can arrive at the mansion early. I want to look over the house before many guests arrive."

Linda kept her promise and next day Nancy received a note from Mrs. Becker.

Tuesday evening Nancy dressed in a becoming aqua evening dress and drove to the luxurious Becker home. She was met at the door by a pleasant-mannered butler.

"Your invitation, please, miss," he requested.

Nancy showed him the note.

"Miss Seeley told us we might expect you," the servant said. "Come in, please."

The Becker home had been beautifully decorated with palms and flowers, screening every corner of the great house. Nancy reflected that they would offer perfect protection for any uninvited guest!

Wandering at will around the first floor, she noted that men in plain clothes had been stationed at all outside doors. Police, no doubt. She was brought up short as she came face to face with Detective Ambrose.

"You here as a guest or to help us?" he asked sarcastically.

"Perhaps both." Nancy laughed.

"Well, you may be sorry you showed up. I'm afraid there'll be trouble."

"You mean the party thief might be here?"

"I'll let you in on something. We picked up a tip from a caterer who served at a house that was robbed. He said to watch for a crook who'll try to palm himself off as a high-brow Englishman. He speaks with an Oxford accent."

"I'll keep an eye out for him."

Nancy moved away. Roaming through the house, she noted the location of various treasures, including a valuable silver tea service.

"But I doubt that a thief would try to steal anything from the first floor," she reasoned. "It's too well guarded."

Learning from Linda Seeley, whom she met in the hall, that the wedding presents were displayed on the second floor, Nancy went upstairs. The gifts had been attractively arranged on long tables in a narrow room with many mirrors.

Although Nancy had attended many fine weddings, this array of silver and crystal took her breath away.

The only guard in evidence was an elderly servant, so frail that he could not possibly defend

himself against a strong assailant. His only protection was a house telephone which she assumed
connected with the kitchen.

"Are you alone here?" Nancy asked dubiously.

"Yes, miss," he responded. "Mrs. Becker in-
structed me not to leave this room until the reception is over and the last guest gone."

Nancy supposed that the old man was a
trusted and faithful servant. Nevertheless, it
seemed to her that it would have been far wiser to
have assigned a policeman to the upper floor.

Deciding to ask Detective Ambrose about it,
she went downstairs again. Nancy could not find
him, for the bridal party had returned from the
church, photographers were busy taking pictures,
and guests were arriving in large numbers.

Hearing a slight commotion at the front entrance, Nancy turned in that direction. Detective
Ambrose was questioning a tall, distinguished-
looking man. As she came closer, Nancy heard
him speak with a pronounced Oxford accent!

"But I mislaid the invitation at my hotel," he
said.

Instantly Nancy guessed what had occurred.
Since the man had appeared without an invitation, the butler had summoned Detective Ambrose.

The newcomer, indignant at being denied
entrance, tapped his gold-handled cane impa-
tiently.

"I perceive that the reception is in progress," he said coldly. "Dashed if I can understand all this bally fuss about an invitation. I have explained to the butler that I was detained at my hotel by Lord Atchfield. Hence the invitation was forgotten. Let me pass."

"Don't be in such a rush," Detective Ambrose advised him rudely. "Your getup and your speech don't fool me."

"My getup? I say, your words mystify me. Mrs. Becker certainly shall hear of this affront!"

"You bet she will!" Detective Ambrose took the man firmly by the arm. "Come along. If a member of the family can identify you, you get in. Otherwise, you're going with me to the police station."

"The police station! I say, old chap, you're making a frightful mistake."

Despite the Englishman's protests, the detective marched him into the house. He asked the butler to bring Mr. Becker to the hall. In a moment the worried father of the bride came from the receiving line.

"This man's trying to get in without an invitation," the detective informed him. "Says his name is Earl Countway."

"The Earl of Countway, Sussex," the guest corrected, bowing slightly. "Sorry to have caused all this trouble, but—"

"I never saw this man before," broke in Mr. Becker.

"Ha!" chortled Detective Ambrose. His grip tightened on the Englishman's arm. "Just as I thought! The Velvet Kid in disguise. Okay, pal, come along! You're going with me for a nice little ride to headquarters."

"I say!" the guest sputtered. "I demand that you notify Mrs. Becker of my presence in this house."

The bride's father had already turned away.

"Come along peaceful-like or I'll put handcuffs on you," the detective threatened the earl. "Get going!"

Nancy vaguely recalled having read a few days before in a New York paper of the arrival in this country of an Earl of Countway. Suppose this man were he and not the thief in disguise!

"Mrs. Becker may have invited him and forgot to tell her husband," Nancy thought.

Determined to check the matter herself, she quickly approached the receiving line and whispered to the bride's mother.

"Do you know the Earl of Countway?"

"Know him! Indeed I do!" exclaimed Mrs. Becker. "He's an old friend. Don't tell me the old darling flew from New York to attend our daughter's reception!"

Mr. Becker was horrified at the turn of events.

Quickly his wife explained that she had read of the earl's arrival and on the spur of the moment had sent him a last-minute invitation.

Together she and her husband followed Nancy to where the detective's car was parked. Mr. Becker grasped the man's arm as his wife greeted the earl and apologized profusely for what had happened.

"We have this young lady to thank," Mrs. Becker said, turning to Nancy. "Since I don't know you, I presume you're helping the Lightner people?"

"Yes, Mrs. Becker."

Detective Ambrose glared at Nancy. Then he muttered, "I was only trying to do my duty, ma'am. We were tipped off to watch for an Englishman, and this guy—I mean his lordship, the earl—fit the bill. Your husband couldn't identify him."

"Of course not. They've never met. I hope you make no further mistakes of this nature, or I shall report you."

Suddenly Nancy realized that if the thief and his accomplices had been waiting for a chance to attend the reception without showing invitations, they had been given a golden opportunity. Both the detective and the butler had been away from the front door for several minutes!

Worried, Nancy returned to the house and hastened to the second floor. Surprisingly, the door to the room in which the wedding gifts were displayed now was closed.

Why? she wondered excitedly. She gently twisted the knob and was even more startled to discover it locked.

"Perhaps one of the plain-clothes men shut the door when the trouble started," she told herself, trying not to think the worst. "But where is the servant who was ordered not to leave here?"

Nancy noticed that a door to an adjoining bedroom stood ajar. She peered inside. Seeing no one there, she tiptoed in.

A velvet curtain screened an entranceway into the locked room. Moving noiselessly to the heavy drapery, Nancy cautiously pulled the folds apart.

Involuntarily she drew back at the sight before her. The elderly servant lay sprawled on the floor, apparently unconscious.

Standing in front of one of the tables on which the wedding silver was displayed was a man in formal summer attire with a velvet hooded mask over his head!

CHAPTER VI

An Anonymous Demand

WITHOUT realizing that she might be running headlong into danger, Nancy rushed from behind the drapery.

The man in the black velvet hood whirled around. Startled, he dropped a dark cloth bag into which he had been stuffing pieces of wedding silver.

"So it's the great girl detective!" the man hissed at her.

The same voice as that of the thief who had mistaken her for someone else at the Hendricks' masquerade!

He made a lunge for her. But she sidestepped him and blocked the exit. Picking up the telephone, she screamed "Help!" into it.

Then, to Nancy's amazement, the thief leaped onto one of the tables, opened a door in back of it, and fled.

Still shouting for help, Nancy took up the pursuit. The man evidently knew every inch of the rambling house. He ran down a back corridor, through a door, and directly to the servants' stairway, which had a door at the foot.

Nancy followed him down, crying, "Stop thief!"

But reaching the foot of the stairs, she found the door locked.

Nancy pounded on it and presently it was opened by a startled maid. In a moment the place was in an uproar with everyone trying to locate the thief. No one had seen him come through the stairway door.

The shouts had attracted Detective Ambrose and the other plain-clothes men. While they went on a search for the thief, Nancy listened to the voice of every man wearing summer formals, hoping to discover among the guests the man who had spoken to her upstairs. She did not find him.

"I'm sure the thief's gone," she reflected. "Maybe I can learn something from that poor old servant."

She went upstairs and found that her first cry of help on the phone had brought a maid to aid the elderly man. Now he had revived and was seated in a chair in the bedroom.

"I don't know how it happened," the servant said. "I never even saw the person who hit me. He sneaked up like a cat from behind."

Detective Ambrose came in at this moment. He reported no success in apprehending the would-be thief.

"At least he didn't get away with anything this time," the policeman remarked. "Our quick work saved the wedding silver."

"Yes, we were lucky," Nancy replied, smiling at the detective's use of the word *our*.

Finding that the servant had no clues to offer, she returned to the reception. The gayety which had prevailed half an hour before was gone from the party.

Nancy remained awhile, departing when the bride left. Reaching home, she was surprised to find Bess Marvin and George Fayne there. They explained that they had waited, hoping to hear her experiences at the reception.

"Who said I had any?" Nancy laughed.

"Why, it's written all over your face," George declared. "Come on. Tell us. Did you have another encounter with the man in the mask?"

"I did," Nancy said with emphasis, and went on to relate how the thief had eluded her.

"Wish I'd been there," George remarked, her eyes dancing. "I'd have helped you hold him, Nancy."

"I could have used a little of your muscle, George. He's a slippery rascal!"

"Aren't you afraid he'll try to get even with you?" Bess asked nervously. "After all, you wrecked his plans tonight, Nancy, and he prob-ably won't forget it, either."

"I'm not worried."

"You and Mrs. Gruen will be in the house alone tonight, won't you?"

"Yes, Dad is still away on a trip. I'm not the least bit afraid, though."

"Well, you should be," Bess insisted. She glanced fearfully out into the dark street. "Even now that awful man may be—"

"Oh, stop it, Bess!" her cousin George cut in. "You'll give Nancy the jitters with all that silly talk. She's right! There's no need to worry—"

At that moment the telephone rang. In the quiet house the unexpected sound was startling.

"It's probably Dad calling me long-distance," Nancy said. "I've been expecting him to phone."

Excusing herself, she went to the hall and lifted the receiver. At first there was no reply to her hello. Then a man's voice, which was not her father's, spoke precisely and with sinister in-flection:

"Nancy Drew, keep out of affairs that aren't your own! If you don't, be prepared to pay the consequences. Another warning, get rid of that hooded mask. Drop it within twenty-four hours over the wall of Hillside Cemetery."

The receiver clicked, indicating the end of the one-way conversation. Nancy tried frantically to trace the call but was told that it must have been made from a dial phone. Bess and George had joined her, aware that something was amiss.

"Was it a threat?" George demanded.

Nancy nodded. "I've been ordered to get rid of the black hooded mask I picked up at Gloria's home."

"Oh, Nancy!" Bess declared, glancing again toward the dark street. "Didn't I tell you? Why did you ever keep the mask?"

George, intrigued by the mysterious telephone call, eagerly offered her services.

"Let me go with you to get rid of the mask, Nancy! Or won't you obey the order?"

"I most certainly will not! I intend to keep that mask unless the police ask me for it."

"Good for you, Nancy!" George approved. "Don't let that man bluff you!"

"Oh, George, what dangerous advice," protested Bess, always fearful that Nancy would involve herself in real trouble. "I think we should stay here with Nancy tonight."

"That's right," agreed George promptly. "With Mr. Drew away, and after that threatening phone call, anything might happen."

"Not with the doors locked and Hannah Gruen in the house." Nancy smiled. "I wish you both would stay tonight, but not to protect me or Mrs. Gruen. We'll be snug and safe in our beds."

"You hope," Bess sighed. "Well, if you're not

afraid, I guess we may as well run along. It's getting late. But do be careful, Nancy."

"Don't make any rash moves without consulting us," George added with a chuckle. "We want to be in on the fun, you know."

After the girls had gone, Nancy sat for a while in the living room, thinking over details of the case. Then, abruptly, she went to a desk drawer and took out the black hooded mask.

As she was gazing at it, Mrs. Gruen came downstairs from her room.

"Nancy, I think you should go to bed," she remarked. Then noticing the object in the girl's hand, she added with a shudder, "Mooning over that sinister thing again! Why don't you burn it up?"

"Burn up my most valuable clue! Oh, I couldn't do that. Anyway, the police might ask for it. This might be the very thing I need to track down the thieves."

Nancy then revealed to the housekeeper that she had been ordered to get rid of the mask.

"Well, obey their wishes. I heard you telling Bess and George about the fracas tonight. The whole thing's too dangerous."

"Now, Hannah, don't get yourself so upset. Please. You know I've never run into a situation yet that I couldn't find a way out of."

"Just you wait, Nancy Drew. Some day you

won't be able to find a way out. I worry all the time about you and your father. Two of a kind!"

"Well, then," returned Nancy, smiling, "there's no need to worry if I'm like Dad. He's never failed to crack a tough case yet!"

The housekeeper merely shook her head. She realized that it was futile to dissuade the girl from pursuing work on a mystery, once she had started.

"What is it now, Nancy? Why are you staring so hard at that mask?" Hannah asked, noting how intently she was looking at the hood.

"It just occurred to me," Nancy replied, "that the thief must have a good reason why he wants this returned. Perhaps it contains some clue he doesn't want me to find."

"How could it?"

"The mask has a thick, padded, white silk lining," Nancy mused.

"Yes, it has."

"Draw the curtains!" Nancy said suddenly. "I have an idea! One which I hope will pay off!"

CHAPTER VII

Strange Numbers

WHILE Mrs. Gruen watched, Nancy ripped out the silk lining of the velvet mask. To her disappointment, nothing had been hidden inside.

"I guess I was wrong," she admitted ruefully. "I thought jewels or something valuable might have been tucked under the padding."

"I'll sew the lining back in," the housekeeper offered. "Not tonight, though. I'm too sleepy. Just leave the mask beside my sewing machine."

As Nancy started to fold the lining, she noticed that some numbers were written on the reverse side.

"What's this?" she wondered aloud. "The number of this mask?"

Carrying it to a brighter light, Nancy studied the numbers. They read: 626 628 71 75.

"What do they mean?" Mrs. Gruen asked.

"I wish I knew," Nancy replied.

"The ink appears fairly fresh," Mrs. Gruen remarked. "Not faded as it would be if the cloth were old."

"The numbers may be a code. I wonder—"

"Better forget the mask tonight and get some sleep," Mrs. Gruen advised. "It's late."

"I'll go to bed soon," Nancy promised, stifling a yawn. "I'm sure Dad will call."

At this moment the telephone rang and Nancy hastened to the hall to answer it. This time it was her father.

"I'm so glad to hear from you. How's everything?" Nancy asked cheerily.

"Fine on this end. How about you?"

His sleuthing daughter reported her work on the case.

"You haven't been idle, I can see that," he praised her.

Nancy then told him of her latest discovery and that the numbers in the mask puzzled her.

"Read them to me," the lawyer suggested.

After Nancy did so, he said, "Very interesting. They sound like dates."

"You mean 626 is June twenty-sixth?"

"Yes. And the last one's the Saturday after the Fourth of July."

"Oh, Dad, you're wonderful. That's probably exactly what they are—dates. Dates for robberies! The woman in the Javanese costume put them in so she wouldn't forget them, or someone wrote them down before giving her the mask so that she would have a record of them."

"Nancy, here's a suggestion. Call the Lightner Entertainment Company in the morning and find out if they coincide with parties they're arranging. But be discreet in asking questions."

"I will!" Nancy assured him. "And, Dad, when are you coming home?"

Mr. Drew said that unless something unexpected came up he would return from Amster the following evening.

"We miss you," she said. "By the way, you're at the Excelsior, aren't you?"

As Nancy said good-by, she heard a creaking sound outside the front door. Thinking someone was arriving, she went to open it, but no one was there.

"My imagination, I guess," she decided, and went up to bed.

Hopeful to have some information for her father by the next evening, Nancy telephoned Linda Seeley at nine o'clock the following morning. Without explaining where she had obtained the dates, she asked if Lightner's had any parties scheduled for them.

"Yes, we do have for the first two you mentioned," Linda answered without hesitation. "I know, because I've worked on them myself. Wait, I'll check the others."

In a moment she returned to say that July first

was on their books, but the office had no record of the fourth one.

"Nancy, if you're still working on the theft, you'd better be wary," she advised hurriedly. "After what happened last night at the reception and later, I'm getting scared."

"What happened later? Did something new develop?"

"Rather!"

"Tell me," Nancy urged.

Still Linda hesitated. "I think someone may be listening on the line," she finally said in a hushed voice. "Hang up. I'll call you back."

Nancy followed instructions. In less than five minutes the telephone rang.

"I'm sorry," Linda apologized. "Maybe I'm acting silly, but I was sure someone was listening in."

"You can't be too careful," Nancy agreed. "Where are you now?"

"I slipped into the back room. I'm using a private line this time, so we can talk safely."

"What were you about to tell me, Linda?"

"That our establishment was robbed of costumes and masks last night!"

"No!"

"Mr. Lightner hasn't reported the theft to the police yet," Linda went on. "I think that he's afraid to because of the publicity. Anyhow, he and Mr. Tombar were together a long while in the private office this morning. They had an argument because I could hear them shouting at each other. But the upshot of it was they didn't report the theft."

"Tell me what was stolen, Linda."

"Mr. Tombar has the inventory, but I know some of the articles that are missing. For one thing, the Indian masks from Mr. Lightner's private office."

"What else?"

"Two valuable masks kept only for exhibition purposes."

Nancy asked her to describe them as best she could.

"They're ancient Greek religious masks," Linda explained. "Actors in those days used them in theatrical productions. One face represents Joy and the other Sorrow."

"I've seen similar ones in museums," Nancy replied, jotting down notes about the missing items. "Don't they have a sort of megaphone arrangement?"

"Yes. The masks have a circular passage for the voice to come through. They were made that way so that the actors' voices would carry in the big outdoor amphitheaters."

"What costumes are missing?" Nancy asked. She was trying to figure out if the thief had been after any special types.

"Oh, I can't tell yet, exactly," Linda replied.

"We're still checking the wardrobe closets. Several black dominoes are gone, though, and some women's disguises."

Nancy wanted to ask more questions, but Linda suddenly warned her that she must end the conversation.

"Mr. Tombar is coming! I hear his voice!" she declared nervously. "He mustn't find me here at this telephone. I'll get in touch with you later."

"Just one thing," Nancy interposed. "Has a masquerade party been scheduled for any of those dates I told you about?"

"No, only other types of parties," Linda whispered. "I've really got to slip away now. Good-by!"

Hanging up the receiver, Nancy sat at the telephone a moment, absorbed in thought. Why had so many masks and costumes been stolen? Did the thieves intend to sell them, or was it their plan to use the disguises in their own work?

"Mr. Tombar will probably point to this robbery as an excuse to discharge Linda," she thought.

The girl's meditation was cut short as she heard Togo, her small terrier, barking excitedly at the window. He had risen up on his hind legs and was scratching at the sill, as if trying to get out.

"Togo, what's wrong with you?" Nancy demanded.

Her pet almost never barked unless he detected an unfriendly dog near by or thought that someone was trying to break into the house.

Mrs. Gruen already had gone to the window. Nancy joined her, peering into the sunny side yard. They glanced around expectantly, but there was no one in sight.

"Togo, you were really fooled this time," Nancy scolded him. "No one's out there."

The little terrier continued to bark, however, not at all convinced by his mistress' words. He ran to the front door, jerking his head and scratching frantically with his paws to tell Nancy that he wanted to go out.

"What can be the matter?" she said, frowning. "I've never seen him so persistent."

She ordered her pet to come away from the door and lie down. To her vexation, the usually obedient Togo paid no attention to her command.

By now he was beside himself, and jumped against the door, turning his head beseechingly to Nancy. She started toward the dog, but whirled around at a sharp exclamation from Hannah.

"Togo *did* sense someone lurking near the window!" the housekeeper declared. "Nancy, I just saw a long, moving shadow fall across the porch."

Nancy dashed for the door. "Then our house *is* being watched!" she cried, recalling the sound that she had heard the night before.

CHAPTER VIII

Trickery

As NANCY opened the door, Togo bounded outside. The little dog raced directly toward the garage, barking furiously.

"He saw someone, all right," Nancy declared. She could see the vague impressions of a man's footprints that led directly to the window near the telephone. "Someone was listening. I'm going to look around outside."

"Don't do it," Mrs. Gruen said nervously. "It may be that thief seeking revenge!"

"In broad daylight?" Nancy laughed.

Telling the housekeeper to watch from the window, she followed the dog to the garage. The building was empty.

Togo ran around the yard, his nose to the ground. Picking up the stranger's scent, he followed it to the street and there became confused.

"Whoever it was, he's gone now, Togo," Nancy

said, calling her pet back into the house. "Good dog! You tried hard."

The housekeeper was greatly concerned by the disturbance.

"Probably it was a member of that Velvet Gang," she remarked. "I suspect the man wanted to get his black hood."

"Now stop worrying," Nancy begged. "If he'd wanted it, he would have tried harder to get it. Nevertheless, I'll get in touch with Chief Denny."

She telephoned, bringing him up to date on all she had learned and asking if she might still retain the mask since her father wanted to see it again.

"All right," the chief said. "So long as we have those dates that's the important thing. Be sure you don't lose the mask," he warned her jokingly.

"I promise."

Mrs. Gruen remained jumpy and Nancy did not leave her. Hours later, when she and Nancy were upstairs, the housekeeper gave a sudden start.

"Listen!" she said tensely. "What was that?"

"Only the front doorbell. I'll go."

"Be careful, Nancy. It may be a trick."

The housekeeper's suspicions were unwarranted. Opening the door, Nancy found a telegraph messenger boy standing there. She took

the envelope which was addressed to her and tore
it open. The wire read:

HAVE FOUND WHAT DATES MEAN.   NO
NEED CONTACT LIGHTNER.   COME MY
HOTEL THIS EVENING.   BRING MASK.

It was signed "Dad."

"Bad news?" Mrs. Gruen asked, hovering near.

"Not exactly," Nancy was rereading the telegram. "This message has me puzzled, though.
Why should Dad ask me to come to Amster when
he expects to arrive home today?"

She offered the telegram to Mrs. Gruen for her
opinion. The woman shrugged.

"Apparently your father has solved the mystery," she said after reading it. "You'll go, of
course."

"I'm wondering if I should."

"Why, Nancy!"

"This telegram may be a hoax."

"That's so," Mrs. Gruen admitted. "I never
thought of that! Well, the only thing to do is to
verify it."

Nancy put in a long-distance call to her father.
The hotel operator informed her that Carson
Drew was not in his room. She assured the girl,
however, that he had not checked out.

His daughter further learned that a telegram
had been sent to her from the hotel, charged to
her father's bill. Turning from the telephone,

Nancy said reassuringly to worried Mrs. Gruen:

"Evidently Dad sent the telegram, so I'll take the mask and meet him."

She got in touch with the railroad station and learned that the only through train from River Heights to Amster left in less than two hours.

"Since Dad wants me there this evening, I'll have to take it," she remarked.

She had barely said this when Togo growled and ran to the door.

"Another eavesdropper!" Hannah Gruen cried, and went outside herself this time.

But there was no one in sight. A car was just pulling away from in front of the house next door. Could the driver have been spying on the Drew home? she wondered. Annoyed and ill at ease she returned to tell Nancy about it.

"Maybe you'd better have Bess and George sleep here tonight," Nancy urged. "I'll call them."

She phoned George and asked her to pick up Bess.

"Be there in fifteen minutes," George promised.

While Hannah Gruen hurriedly pressed a suit for Nancy, the girl brought an overnight bag from the attic.

"I mustn't forget to pack the black mask," she told herself. "Dad especially asked for it—I can't imagine why."

Bess and George arrived before she had decided

what clothes to take with her. They were astonished to learn that she was leaving at once for Amster.

"Nancy, you're not going alone!" George protested. "Why, someone might try to snatch that mask from you."

"It does worry me a little," Nancy admitted. "The mask is my only important clue. I'd hate to lose it."

"Why go?" Bess asked.

"Dad is expecting me."

"He wouldn't want you to take any risks," George declared. "And I have a hunch this thing isn't quite on the level."

"Me too," Bess added. "I almost wish we were going instead of you. How about it?"

"I wish you could, girls, but—"

George snapped her fingers. "That gives me an idea. It will make everything safe as a bank vault!"

Nancy was folding the black velvet mask into the open traveling case, but she looked up startled. "What's your idea?"

"I'll masquerade as you! I can wear your clothes and carry your bag."

"But what about your hair?" Nancy asked, surveying George's dark close-cut bob.

"That's where the Lightner Entertainment Company comes in. I'll rent a blond wig for me and a black one for you."

Nancy was thoughtful. The idea appealed to her, and if the girls' hunches were right, she might even catch the person who wanted the mask back!

"Well, what say?" George prodded.

"There's one drawback," said Nancy. "With eavesdroppers around I think none of us should rent the wigs."

"It's easy to solve that one." George looked over Nancy's shoulder. "Here's the person to do it. Hello, Mrs. Gruen."

George flew to the phone and called Mrs. Fayne and Mrs. Marvin, who gave their permission for the girls to go. Then, before the housekeeper knew what was happening, she was in a taxi and on her way to the Lightner Entertainment Company.

Meanwhile, it was decided that the mask would be carried in Bess's bag. As soon as Mrs. Gruen returned with the wigs and the train tickets, George took Nancy's initialed suitcase and the cousins left to return home to dress for the trip.

"Hurry! There's not much time!" Nancy called to them. "And, Bess, take a bag without initials. I will too."

Bess and Nancy met on the station platform a short while afterward.

"If George misses the train, I'll never forgive her," Bess remarked as they looked about anxiously.

It was only two minutes to train time. A long,

shrill whistle warned that it was nearing the station.

Nancy was hopefully watching an approaching cab. It careened up to the platform. To the relief of the two girls, George leaped out.

"Why, Nancy, she looks like your twin!" Bess said in an undertone. "Or at least the way you looked before you changed yourself into George Fayne!"

"Sh!" Nancy warned. "Not so loud or someone will hear you. And don't watch George as she boards the train."

By prearrangement she and Bess sat down near the rear of the second coach. Soon George came in with her luggage. In seating herself at the front of the car, she set the case so that the initials N.D. were plainly visible to anyone passing through the aisle.

"I hope the trick works," Bess whispered to Nancy.

"It will," she predicted.

She nudged her friend to draw attention to three passengers who had entered the car directly behind George. One was a dark-eyed, sullen-looking woman in smartly tailored clothes. She was accompanied by two men.

They scrutinized George, who pretended to be thumbing through a magazine. Then their gaze wandered down the aisle to Nancy and Bess.

The woman and one of the men sat down in the double seat across the aisle from George.

The second man came down the aisle, taking a seat directly in front of Bess and Nancy. This was an unforeseen complication, for now they were unable to talk without fear of being over-heard.

Nancy and Bess, however, were jubilant. They were certain their ruse had worked!

The three passengers easily might have chosen other seats, for there were several empty ones in the car. Instead, two had deliberately sat near the girl they thought was Nancy, and the third had probably stationed himself to listen to Nancy and Bess.

Bess leaned over and whispered into Nancy's ear, "I wonder if they're members of the Velvet Mask Gang?"

"Time will tell," she replied in a low voice.

Nancy settled back in her seat and opened a magazine but did not read.

The man in the seat ahead paid no attention to the other passengers and devoted himself to a copy of a New York newspaper.

Half an hour later the conductor called out the name of a small but busy town. Nancy noticed that the stranger had put aside his newspaper. Was he going to leave the train? Had she been entirely mistaken about him?

Nancy and Bess did not venture even a whispered remark. Nevertheless, they exchanged glances.

The train began to slow down for the station. Nancy and Bess looked up to see what the couple across the aisle from George would do.

The girls were just in time to see the dark-haired woman arise, step across the aisle, and bend over George. When she straightened, the masquerading "Nancy Drew" had slumped over, apparently in a faint!

CHAPTER IX

Kidnaped

"OH, DEAR, our daughter is ill," the strange woman proclaimed in a voice loud enough for Nancy and Bess to hear. "We must get her off the train at once!"

By this time they had reached the station. The woman seized the suitcase with the initials N.D. Her companion gathered George up in his arms, carrying her toward the front exit.

Nancy and Bess were shocked. Dreadfully alarmed, they grabbed their overnight bags and started down the aisle in pursuit. But their way was immediately blocked by the man who had seated himself directly ahead of them.

"Quick! Let us pass!" Nancy said.

"What's the hurry, sister?" he asked, not moving, and swaying from side to side to prevent their pushing past him.

Nancy knew now why he had taken that particular seat. George's kidnaping had been planned—her abductors wanted no interference!

"Let us through!" Bess ordered. "Our friend up there is ill!"

"There's plenty of time, girlie."

"No, there isn't," Bess fairly yelled. "That girl up there. She—"

"The rear exit!" Nancy whispered.

She wheeled and Bess followed her. The man turned too. He overtook them just as they reached the back of the car and roughly pushed them aside so that he might open the door and reach the vestibule first. Planting himself directly in front of the steps he again blocked their way.

"Now don't get mad," he said in a wheedling voice. "You seem to be in a big hurry. I was hopin' to get acquainted with the two of you."

"Get out of our way!" Nancy demanded.

Enraged, she and Bess both sprang at the man and shoved him aside. They leaped down the steps and, looking up the platform, realized why they had been delayed in leaving the train. The unconscious George had been put into a waiting automobile. As Nancy and Bess ran toward it, the car raced away from the station!

"We must get that policeman and chase them!" Nancy cried, seeing an officer standing back of the station. "And, Bess, don't let that man from the train get away!"

Poor Bess! She was so frightened that she was trembling. But as Nancy raced for the officer, Bess turned back and tried to find him. To her horror he too was driving away, but in a different direction from the one which the kidnap car had taken.

In the meanwhile, George was slowly regaining consciousness. But she could not move a single muscle, not even those of her eyelids. As if from a great distance she heard a man say:

"Well done. This time Nancy Drew wasn't so smart. You got the mask?"

"It should be in her suitcase," a woman's voice informed him.

"Then dig it out fast! We haven't got all day, you know. It has to be burned before this one comes to. Then we'll make her talk."

"The whiff I gave her'll easily last that long," the woman said.

"Cut the chatter and get out that mask!"

George could hear her snapping the locks on the suitcase. Rapidly she went through the few garments it contained.

"Something's wrong," the woman muttered. "It's not here."

"What!" the man thundered.

"Look at this blouse with the initials G.F. This girl isn't Nancy Drew!"

"Idiot!" another man stormed. "Are you sure?"

"But we thought from the suitcase and her hair—"

"You thought!" the man mocked her. "You mean you don't think! I'll take a look at the girl myself."

He pulled the car into a clump of bushes at the side of the road. Alighting, the driver walked around to the back seat and stared at the seemingly sleeping George.

"She's a phony," he said in a rasping voice. "Look! She's wearing a wig!" he cried, snatching it off. "You two dunces rode with her on the train but were too dumb to see through it."

"She kept her hat on," the woman tried to excuse herself.

"Besides," said her companion, "she held a magazine in front of her face most of the time."

"You've been outwitted, and by Nancy Drew too!" the other man yelled. "No telling what she's done about those dates in the velvet mask by this time. We're in a spot. To top it off, this girl's coming around," he observed as George stirred. "She'll be a nuisance to us. Blindfold her!"

George tried to open her eyes but she could not do it. Her eyelids felt so very, very heavy. The effort to raise them was too great.

"Blindfold her, I said!" the man roared.

A handkerchief was bound tightly across

George's eyes. She tried hard to resist but could not! The girl realized that she was in danger, but even this thought failed to rouse her from the stupor into which she had fallen.

"Where is the black velvet hood?" the woman hissed in her ear. "What did Nancy Drew do with it?"

There was no answer. Even had George wanted to, she would have been unable to respond. Her memory was so befogged at the moment that the woman's question was a meaningless jumble of words.

"I'll make her tell the truth," one of the men said in an ominous tone. "This little—er—potion will do the trick. I keep it on hand for just such emergencies."

George vaguely felt something sting her arm. There was silence for a short while, then the man ordered:

"Now talk."

George felt herself becoming drowsy all over again, and a fresh sensation of numbness spread through her limbs.

"You gave her too big a dose," the woman cried, annoyed. "Who's the dunce this time! Can't you see she's going under again?"

"Yeah," broke in the other man. "A lot of good she'll do us now!"

"Okay, okay," growled their companion. "So

I gave her too much. We'd just better get out of here fast before the Drew dame puts the cops on us."

"Listen! A car's coming!" cried the woman shrilly. "Let's get rid of the girl and her bag and scram!"

"Open the door! Quick!" commanded one of the men tersely.

Hastily George's captors lifted her out and propped her back of a tree, together with Nancy's suitcase and her own handbag.

"Now, young lady, how do you like that?" the woman sneered.

She grasped George's arm tightly for an instant, whispering a threat into her ear. Even dazed as George was, the words burned deeply into her brain.

"I advise you not to forget!" the woman warned with a harsh laugh.

"Come on! Hurry!" the driver cried.

The couple jumped back into the car. It roared away in a cloud of dust. George, left alone, gave a sigh and sank back in a deep sleep.

CHAPTER X

A Chase

FRIGHTENED by the bold manner in which George Fayne had been abducted, Nancy and Bess immediately summoned the station policeman. Excitedly they revealed what had happened, urging him to help them rescue George.

"Did you get the license number of the car that took your friend away?" the officer asked.

Both shook their heads.

"It was a brown sedan," Nancy recalled. "It turned at the first corner. Can't you chase it? We'll go with you."

"That street leads into the rural area," he replied. "It's out of my territory."

"But we have to do something!" Bess wailed.

"I can't leave here, but I'll report it," the policeman said. "Did you notice anything else?" he asked.

"No–o," Nancy replied. "That is, nothing that will help us now."

Actually she had made one other fleeting observation. Just as the car crossed the railroad tracks, she had seen one of the kidnapers drop a small object. From a distance, it had appeared to be a shiny metal disk. Nancy wanted to search for it, but just now there was no time, and moreover another train was coming in.

"If that car has taken the Old Mill Road, it's a case for the state police," the officer said. "I'll call 'em."

Nancy was impatient about the delay in following the kidnapers, nevertheless there was nothing she could do but wait. Finally the officer came from the booth.

"Okay, they'll try to pick up the trail," he reported, "but they'd like you girls along."

"Where do we meet them?" Nancy asked, fidgety that time was passing and George was getting farther away.

"Their headquarters are on Old Mill Road. I'll take you that far."

The girls picked up their overnight bags and jumped into his car, which sped to the outskirts of town. There was no sign of the brown sedan.

They transferred to a waiting state police car containing two officers who introduced themselves as Lieutenants Connolly and Whyte. Nancy and Bess told their story in more detail.

"The Velvet Gang, eh?" Whyte said. "This is serious."

The four riders kept a sharp lookout for the thieves' car. There was no way of knowing whether or not they had taken the right route as they followed the winding, dusty Old Mill Road. Fresh tire tracks indicated that a car had passed that way recently, but whether it was the brown sedan they had no way of knowing.

Presently Whyte radioed to headquarters, reporting failure so far and asking if there was any news from surrounding towns which had been alerted. He learned that the abductors had not been picked up.

The officer had just replaced his radiophone when Nancy cried out, "Stop!" Her alert eyes had caught sight of a girl propped against a tree at the edge of a woods.

"It's George!"

The blond wig was gone and she appeared to be only semiconscious. Nancy and Bess leaped from the car and ran to her. As they shook her gently, George opened her eyes.

"Nancy! Bess!" she murmured, and started weeping hysterically on Nancy's shoulder.

"Everything's all right, George," Nancy said, comforting her.

"What happened?" Bess asked as she too slipped a protective arm about the trembling girl's waist.

It was so unlike George to give way to her feelings with tears.

"That woman—she said such dreadful things—"

"Don't let it upset you," Bess advised. "You're safe and unharmed. That's all that matters."

"No, no! It's not all that matters," George contradicted her cousin, her words thick and barely audible. "Nancy must give up the case."

"Give it up?" Nancy echoed in disbelief. "Why, George! It's astounding to hear you suggest such a thing! You're the one who has been urging me to solve it."

"I was wrong. You'll get hurt, Nancy. You mustn't do it."

The troopers had come up and were listening to the girls' conversation. Now Lieutenant Whyte asked what was meant by Nancy solving the case. Quickly Bess gave a glowing account of her friend's ability as a detective.

"That's amazing," he remarked. "If you solve the mystery of the party thieves, my hat's off to you."

"But she mustn't do any more work on it," George mumbled.

Nancy and Bess exchanged glances. This was not the old George Fayne! She certainly had been badly frightened, but after a good night's sleep she would be her normal self.

Officer Whyte knelt down beside George, and

taking her wrist counted the girl's pulse beat. He puckered his brow.

"Tell me exactly what happened," he said kindly.

"I—I don't know. That woman leaned over me in the train. I smelled something very sweet on her handkerchief—funny perfume—and then I fainted."

"When did you wake up?" Whyte asked.

"I don't know. What time is it?"

"I mean was it while you were in the woman's car or after?" the officer questioned.

"A man was just carrying me out of it. I—oh!"

George stopped speaking to gaze at an angry-looking spot on one arm. The policeman also was staring at it.

"I've been bitten," she said.

"That may not be an insect bite," he said gravely. "I believe those thieves used a needle and gave you a hypo of something."

Bess shrieked. "Oh, George, maybe they—they—"

"No, it's not that bad," Whyte said. "They thought Miss Fayne was a detective who was in their way. We'll take her to a doctor for a checkup."

When they returned to town George was questioned and examined by the police surgeon. He said that it was impossible to tell what drug had been administered to the girl but advised that she go home and stay in bed for a few days.

"I'll phone Mother to come and get us," Bess offered.

Meanwhile, Nancy telephoned her father's hotel to explain the delay. To her amazement, she learned that he had checked out late that morning.

"Then the telegram *was* a hoax," she thought. "Those people certainly are clever. They were eavesdropping at my house and heard all our plans!"

Asking the operator to connect her with the Drew home, Nancy found out that her father had come back by plane and was in his office. She called him there and told him what had happened.

"I don't like this at all," he said. "That gang is dangerous. You'd better forget the whole thing," the lawyer advised.

"But, Dad, you gave me a job to do for you and I want to finish it!" Nancy protested. "I can't leave it now!"

"Well, all right. But do your sleuthing in safe places. You'll be home tonight?"

"Yes, Dad."

While waiting for Mrs. Marvin to arrive, Nancy decided to go to the railroad station and search for the object she thought she had seen one of George's abductors drop from his car. She mentioned it to the other girls.

"Oh, Nancy, do you have to?" George said weakly. "Please don't do another thing about those awful people."

Nancy looked at her, about to say that if it would worry her too much she would not go. But George had dropped off to sleep on the couch in the police physician's office.

"I'll be back before George wakes up," Nancy whispered to Bess and left the room.

Going directly to the railroad station, she spent twenty minutes searching along the tracks. Just as Nancy was about to give up, her efforts were rewarded. Beside one of the steel rails she found a rectangular metal tag.

Nancy immediately recognized it as a charge plate issued by department stores. The names and numbers on the plate had been flattened by a train passing over them, but the words "Tay" and "House Acc" were visible.

"Tay," Nancy mused. "I wonder if that could be Taylor's in River Heights? Maybe one of the thieves works there! Tomorrow I'll ask their credit manager if he can identify this house account charge plate."

As she had hoped, George was still drowsy when Nancy returned to the doctor's office. Mrs. Marvin arrived in a little while and was very much concerned when she heard what had happened. The physician assured her that the girl was all right to travel but would probably sleep all the way home.

What the doctor had predicted almost turned out to be true, but George awoke as the others were discussing the subject of masks. She seemed to pay no attention, staring into space out the window. Thinking to divert the girl's attention from herself, Nancy said:

"George, I've been reading a lot about masks. Their history is fascinating. Did you know that among savage people masks are used to frighten away demons?"

"Oh!" said George.

"Masks do play an important role in most ceremonials," Mrs. Marvin nodded. "Priest-doctors and medicine men use them and so do conjurers."

"The ancient Romans made masks of wax," Nancy went on. "And among the Egyptian ruins some have been found made of thin gold plate. Some were called death masks—"

"Must you talk about such horrible things?" George broke in with a shudder. "Nancy, you are positively morbid!"

"I'm sorry," Nancy apologized.

"Let's not talk about masks," George pleaded, twisting her handkerchief. "We—we've had enough of them for all time! I never want to hear of them again. And I hope you'll forget them too."

The distasteful subject was not mentioned again during the remainder of the trip to River Heights. George herself had little to say. Though she insisted that she felt fairly well, her face remained pale and she was shaky.

George's alternate periods of morose silence and fretfulness deeply concerned her friends. This was not the old George!

Nancy did not see her the next day, for Mrs. Fayne kept her daughter in bed as the doctor had suggested. She reported that George had not slept well and had talked incoherently in her dreams, mostly about the Velvet Gang.

"Poor George!" Nancy thought unhappily. "It's really my fault too! I never should have allowed her to masquerade as me."

On her way to see the credit manager of the Taylor Department Store, Nancy thought continuously of the thieves' activities. Since the night of the Becker wedding, no more robberies had been reported.

Yet not for a moment did Nancy believe that the thieves had left the vicinity. When the proper time arrived, they would strike again—possibly on the days indicated in the lining of the black hood.

Nancy was admitted to the office of Mr. Johnson, the credit manager of Taylor's. Without telling him of the previous day's experience, she mentioned a possible tie-in between the party thieves and the plate she carried.

"I'm almost convinced that it may be a helpful clue in tracking down one of the members of that gang," Nancy concluded, and held out the defaced metal plate.

Upon seeing it, the credit manager frowned. He examined the plate carefully.

"It's one of ours all right," he said. "This was issued to an employee. But to tell you his or her name—that's quite impossible."

"Impossible?" Nancy asked, disappointed. "Why, Mr. Johnson?"

"Miss Drew," was the rather impatient reply, "Taylor's is a very large store. We have several hundred employees. At least a hundred and fifty charge plates have been issued to them."

"You must have a record of every one," Nancy reminded him.

"We have. But the number of this plate has been obliterated. I couldn't interview a hundred and fifty of our workers on such slim evidence. I'd like to assist you, Miss Drew, but to comply with your request would take entirely too much time."

"Even if the owner of this plate were a dangerous, wanted thief?"

Mr. Johnson arose, plainly indicating that he did not wish to discuss the matter any further. His face red from the insinuation in her remark, he said icily:

"Taylor Brothers certainly does not employ people of this type. Good day!"

CHAPTER XI

The Woman of Mystery

IT WAS with a sinking heart that Nancy started for the door. But she was not one to give up easily. Though Mr. Johnson was dismissing her, she did not take his refusal as final.

"A clever person with a police record may have slipped into your employ," she countered.

"That's possible of course," he agreed, realizing that he had been rather abrupt with Nancy. "I'd like to co-operate, Miss Drew. But as I've explained, it would mean endless work to find the owner of this particular plate."

"I know how the checkup could be made without very much work," Nancy said.

"How?"

"Just this. Ask all your employees to turn in their plates on a pretext of changing them. Naturally the person who lost this one wouldn't be able to."

Mr. Johnson paused near the door and considered the suggestion.

"Such a procedure would establish the honesty of your clerks and other employees," Nancy pressed her point.

Finally the credit manager admitted that Nancy's proposal could be carried out with a minimum of trouble.

"You present you arguments very well, Miss Drew." He smiled. "I'll do it, even though it does inconvenience us."

Satisfied that she had done all she could to find out who the owner of the charge plate was, Nancy next dropped in at her father's law office. He was dictating a letter to his secretary, but promptly put aside the task.

"Nothing new to report," he anticipated her questions. "Mr. Lightner came in to see me this morning. He's still worried about those threatened lawsuits. We're stalling for time. And what's your news?"

Nancy told him, then said she was going to follow Mr. Tombar that noon when he went to lunch.

"But only at a safe distance," the lawyer cautioned. "And suppose you tell me what you hope to find out."

Nancy told him about seeing Tombar bring a package from the entertainment company the same morning the telltale cloak disappeared.

"He shook me off his trail rather pointedly when I followed him," she said. "And he's perfectly horrid about Linda without any reason, it seems to me. She's a fine girl and I'm sure above suspicion. She's very smart, too. Maybe he's afraid she'll find out something about him that he doesn't want her to know.

"And, Dad, about that big robbery of costumes and masks from the company—it wouldn't surprise me if Mr. Tombar knows more about it than he's telling."

"That's a harsh accusation, Nancy," her father said. "Better keep your suspicions to yourself until you have some evidence to back them up."

"I promise, Dad."

Nancy phoned Linda Seeley who told her that Mr. Tombar had not come in that day.

"And the mysterious torn black cloak has never been returned," Linda reported. "But I have something else to tell you," she said. "Come over at noontime, will you?"

"Meet you at the drugstore soda counter," Nancy promised.

At noon the two girls met at the fountain and sat down side by side. Linda seemed almost happy and said that everything was going well at the Lightner Entertainment Company.

"But I suppose something could happen at any time. Nancy, how would you like to attend a musicale?"

"When?"

"Tomorrow afternoon. At the Elkin home on Kenwood Boulevard. The affair will be very ritzy. It's to introduce the French singer, Madame de Velleaux, and there'll be wonderful refreshments, too."

Nancy giggled. "You mean you're bound to enjoy one thing or the other? Is your company in charge?"

"Yes, and I can get you an invitation if you're interested. I'll be there."

Nancy decided instantly. She would enjoy the concert and there was the possibility that one of the party thieves might put in an appearance.

"I'd like to go," she said. "Where shall I meet you, Linda?"

"I may have to go early," the other replied. "Tell you what! I'll send your invitation by special messenger. Then if I'm held up, you won't be kept waiting at the door."

The next day Nancy consulted Hannah Gruen about what to wear.

"Oh, the pink-flowered dress, by all means. And the pink hat with the black velvet bow," the housekeeper said. "And mind you, Nancy, listen to the music and don't get mixed up with any more of those thieves."

Upon reaching the Elkin home, in its attractive setting, Nancy presented her invitation to the butler at the front entrance. The hall and living room where the concert was to be held were richly furnished and held many priceless art objects. So far as the girl could observe, there was not a single plain-clothes man on duty.

Avoiding the music room, which was jammed with chattering women, Nancy lingered near the front door so that she could scrutinize all new arrivals. A few minutes later she caught sight of Peter Tombar. He saw her at the same moment and came over to chat.

"Well, well," he said with unpleasant and false geniality, "fancy meeting you here, Miss Drew! I thought girls your age were only interested in dance music and the latest hit tunes. So you are an admirer of Madame de Velleaux?"

"I've never heard her sing," Nancy replied. Is Linda Seeley here?" she asked.

Mr. Tombar shot Nancy a quick glance. The girl did not betray by her expression that her remark was intended to have a double meaning.

"Linda isn't coming," Mr. Tombar said shortly.

"Is she ill?"

"No. She was needed elsewhere. I sent her to another house. I'm taking over here myself."

Nancy remained silent, wondering whether the excuse he had given was really what lay behind Linda's failure to appear.

"How did you get in?" Mr. Tombar asked Nancy abruptly.

"By invitation."

"And where'd you get the invitation?" the man growled. "Your name wasn't on the guest list."

"No?" Nancy smiled sweetly. "Perhaps you didn't look carefully enough."

Deciding not to give the man an opportunity to question her further, Nancy sauntered away. She entered the music room and seated herself in the last row near the door.

After Nancy had sat there long enough to make it appear that she had come only to hear the concert, she decided to start her sleuthing. Tiptoeing from the room, Nancy stood in the main hall a moment. The other rooms on the lower floor appeared to be deserted. Meeting one of the maids, she asked her if she knew what had become of the man from the Lightner Entertainment Company.

"No, miss, I don't," the maid replied. "I've been upstairs. The only person up there is the sick lady."

"Someone ill?"

"Yes, miss. One of the guests. She was taken sick just a few minutes ago and asked me to fetch her a cup of tea from the kitchen. I'm getting it now."

"Where is the lady?"

"In the bedroom where the guests left their coats. She took sick awful quick. Soon after the musicale started."

The maid hastened on to the kitchen. Nancy hesitated a moment, mulling over the information. Was the woman really ill? The errand might have been a way for her to get rid of the maid!

"I'll offer to help and see if the story's true," Nancy thought, quietly mounting the carpeted stairway.

So silent was the girl's approach that she reached the bedroom and opened the partly closed door without any warning of her arrival. A slim woman, in a dark-blue dress which clung to her shapely hips, stood at the dresser. She had her back to the door and was hurriedly removing jewelry from the top drawer!

In the mirror Nancy caught a fleeting glimpse of a hard, brazen face. She knew instantly that she had seen the woman some place. But where? One of George's abductors? No. The Hendricks' ball perhaps? Yes, that was it! This was the woman who had worn the Javanese costume!

Now Nancy had caught her red-handed in the act of stealing! She must bar the exit and call for help.

Before she could make a move, Nancy suddenly felt herself grasped from behind by an arm. As she attempted to squirm around, a hand was pressed over her eyes.

"You'd better not make a peep," came the

woman's harsh voice. "Or else—" she added ominously.

Although Nancy's first impulse had been to cry out, she had refrained. For even without the threat just uttered, she knew very well that these thieves would stop at nothing to gain their ends.

Now she was shoved roughly into the room. Although Nancy struggled with all her might, she was pushed, face down, among the wraps on the bed and held there in a viselike grip. She was unable to move an inch.

"Good work!" she heard the woman exclaim. "Serves the little sneak right!"

"I jolly well perceived something might be amiss up here," replied the man, speaking with an exaggerated Oxford accent.

Still maintaining a tight hold on Nancy, her captor chuckled softly.

"I fancy she'll not interfere again soon," he added.

With that, he rolled the bedspread tightly around Nancy and piled a number of coats on top of her.

"Give it to her good," cried the woman. "Make sure she won't meddle any more!"

"No time, my deah," the man answered. "We shall be forced to make a hasty exit. The maid is returning."

"Then cut out that silly lingo and let's get out of here—but fast!" the woman muttered.

Nancy used every muscle in a frantic effort to free herself. A wave of panic seized her as she fought desperately for breath in the rolled-up bedspread.

Just when she thought she surely would suffocate, the man suddenly released his hold. He and the woman raced from the room.

CHAPTER XII

A Job As Spy

NANCY struggled to untangle herself from the heavy bedspread and its burden of coats. When she finally got to her feet and looked in the hall, the man and woman had disappeared.

Just then the maid who had gone for the tea opened a door from a back stairway and walked forward.

"Save us!" she exclaimed, staring at Nancy. "What happened to you?"

For the first time Nancy realized how disheveled she must look. Her pretty pink-flowered dress was torn and rumpled. Her hair was mussed and the pink hat lay on the floor.

"The woman who pretended to be ill was a thief! She and some man tried to smother me."

"Oh, goodness!" The maid nearly dropped the tea tray.

"Did you see anyone running out?"

"No, miss."

"Maybe they're hiding in one of the bedrooms. Come on.   Let's look for them!"

"I'm a-scared to," the maid refused.

"Then you stay here and I'll do it," Nancy said.   "Don't let anyone take a wrap from this room until I return."

"Everything's in an awful mess."

"Try to straighten things out a bit," Nancy advised as she started away.

One by one she searched the bedrooms, looking in closets and every other possible hiding place. Satisfied that no one remained upstairs, she went hastily to the ground floor.

All was serene, with no one lurking about.   In the kitchen she found Mr. Tombar directing the caterers.

"Guests aren't allowed in here," he said to her icily.   "What's the big idea?"

Nancy was not intimidated by his boorish manner.   "I came to get a chicken sandwich," she said, picking one up from a tray.   "I'm simply starved."

She smiled and closed the door.   At this moment a burst of applause from the music room indicated that the musicale was just ending. A moment later the guests began leaving the room and going toward the attractive dining room for tea.

Nancy located the hostess, introduced herself,

told why she was there and whispered what had happened.

"I don't know whether that woman took anything or not," she said. "Perhaps you'd better check."

Together they went upstairs. Mrs. Elkin said that she disliked parties with detectives standing around and had refused to have any there this afternoon.

"Every person on my list is a friend," she said. "I don't see how a thief could have slipped in."

Mrs. Elkin was convinced otherwise when she discovered that several pieces of valuable jewelry were missing and immediately called the police.

"I may have a clue," Nancy spoke up. "Possibly the woman left a coat here that will identify her."

At Mrs. Elkin's request a woman detective not in uniform was sent over from headquarters to take charge of the coats. The hostess was asked, however, to identify each guest as she came to ask for hers.

Finally all of the coats had been claimed except one long blue one with large pockets. Nancy checked to see if any guests were left downstairs. She returned to say everyone had departed.

"The owner is not coming for this coat, that's evident!" she said. "My guess is that it was worn by the thief."

Picking up the garment, Nancy examined it for

clues. In one pocket was a make-up kit. The other pocket contained a velvet hooded mask!

The policewoman ripped the lining of the coat. Nothing had been hidden inside, and the garment had no marks of identification. Store and dry cleaning marks had been removed.

"I'll take this coat and mask to headquarters with me," the woman said.

After Nancy reached home, Linda Seeley telephoned to apologize for her failure to attend the musicale.

"Mr. Tombar sent me on a trifling errand and took over himself," she said. "I guess he thought that I wasn't capable of handling the affair."

Nancy remarked that Mr. Tombar himself had not performed too efficiently and told of the robbery.

"Oh, how dreadful!" Linda cried.

After the phone call, Nancy sat lost in thought. She was getting nowhere on the case. Suddenly an idea came to her. She would have a chemical analysis made of the ink notations which she had discovered on the lining of the hooded mask she had.

In the morning she went to a laboratory technician and was informed that the fluid used was rather uncommon. It was new and sold exclusively for marking garments.

"Then any number of dry cleaners might have similar ink?" Nancy asked.

"Not necessarily," she was told. "You'll not find many River Heights plants that use this particular type of ink. It's pretty expensive."

Nancy was excited. Did the Lightner Entertainment Company use it? she wondered. At noon she managed to meet Linda at the drugstore and asked her how costumes and masks were marked by the firm.

"Oh, we use a special indelible ink that lasts forever," Linda replied.

"Could you let me see a bottle of it?"

"Why, I guess so. How soon do you want it, Nancy?"

"Right away if I can have it."

"Wait here, and I'll see if I can slip one out of the supply room," Linda said. "It's safe enough if Bright-Eyes Tombar doesn't see me."

Ten minutes later the girl returned with the bottle of ink, wrapped in an office envelope. As she gave it to Nancy, Peter Tombar entered the drugstore.

He could not possibly have known what the fat envelope contained, for Nancy thrust it quickly into her handbag. Nevertheless, he regarded the two girls suspiciously. Linda, becoming confused by his unfriendly scrutiny, acted rather guilty.

Mr. Tombar walked over to the lunch counter. He looked pointedly at the wall clock.

"Miss Seeley, you are five minutes over your lunch hour," he said.

"I'm sorry, Mr. Tombar. I—I was just leaving."

"Leaving? I thought you were just coming. Didn't you hand—"

"Are you eating here?" Nancy broke in pointedly.

Mr. Tombar glared at her but did not reply. Linda took advantage of the moment to escape from the drugstore.

Nancy regretted the meeting with Mr. Tombar. He could not possibly know what Linda had given her, but he might try to find out. She must work fast.

No sooner had Mr. Tombar left the drugstore than Nancy returned to the laboratory. She gave the chemist the bottle of ink for analysis and waited for his report.

Finally it came. She was informed that the ink was identical with that used on the inside of the lining of the hooded mask.

"What a clue!" Nancy thought, and hurried from the shop.

On Sunday she told her father of her suspicions about the ink.

"Now I'm positive someone at Lightner's is a member of the gang," she said. "If I could only work there a few days, I could watch everyone."

"Well, can't it be arranged? You're on good terms with Linda. Couldn't you help her with the office filing, or something of the sort? I'm sure that Mr. Lightner would give his permission if I ask him."

Nancy's father promptly put in a call to the man's home. After a brief conversation, he hung up.

"It's all settled," Mr. Drew reported to his daughter. "Mr. Lightner was most agreeable to the suggestion."

"That's fine, Dad," responded Nancy. "Now perhaps I'll unearth a definite clue by being right on the spot from morning till closing time."

Nancy appeared punctually at the Lightner Entertainment Company at nine o'clock Monday morning. She noted, with some amusement, Mr. Tombar's reaction to seeing her there. After his first unfriendly glare, he ignored Nancy pointedly. But he was heard to say in disgruntled tones that business was bad enough without hiring new clerks.

Nancy spent an uneventful morning sorting letters and rearranging a file on the history of masks. However, whenever she was about to seize an opportunity for slipping into the storerooms to look for any evidence, Mr. Tombar would suddenly appear again.

"Hm," the girl remarked to herself. "He may not be speaking to me, but he's surely keeping an eye on my whereabouts."

She decided to wait until later before making any more attempts to enter the storerooms.

"I'll hold off until lunchtime," Nancy thought. "While he's out, I can do some looking around."

She even resolved to forego her own noontime meal, in order to take advantage of Mr. Tombar's absence then.

But when twelve o'clock came, the assistant manager did not leave, nor did he at one. To Nancy's dismay, she observed him eating sandwiches right at his desk.

"Evidently he doesn't intend to budge from here today," Nancy told herself.

This proved to be true, for as Mr. Tombar ate wolfishly, he kept an eagle eye upon the office staff. By late afternoon Nancy was both weary and weak from hunger. Her eyes ached from the tedious filing, and she was discouraged.

When five o'clock came, Nancy left the Lightner offices without seeing Linda. She was sure of one thing: Mr. Tombar must have suspected that she was there for the purpose of sleuthing.

Nancy was not surprised the next morning to receive an urgent telephone call from Linda at eight o'clock.

"It's happened!" the girl announced dramatically. "And I don't know what to do!"

"Another robbery?" Nancy gasped.

"No, not that. I've been discharged!"

CHAPTER XIII

A New Ruse

LINDA poured out the story of why she had been discharged. Mr. Tombar, she told Nancy, had not given her any chance to explain.

"He made an inventory check late yesterday and discovered the ink missing," the girl related. "Just a single little bottle that was opened without his permission! But did he ever make a fuss! He suspected me right away."

"You didn't tell him you lent me the ink?"

"No, but from the way he questioned me, I think he guessed it. Anyway, he made me admit that I had taken the bottle from the shelf. I offered to pay for a full one, but he wouldn't even listen. He just told me I was through working there."

"Now, Linda, don't feel too bad," Nancy comforted her. "I promised to help you, didn't I?"

"Yes, but—"

"I will too," Nancy announced confidently. "Take it easy for a few days and I'll help you to get your job back or find another. A better one where there will be no Mr. Tombar."

"Oh, Nancy," Linda thanked her. "You're so kind. I won't forget how good you've been to me!"

Though Nancy sounded lighthearted, she was troubled. Now that Linda had been discharged she would have no listening post for information at the entertainment company. To make matters worse, Mr. Lightner himself called in a few minutes to say that affairs at the office were a bit confused at the moment and perhaps Nancy had better not return to work there since Linda was gone.

"I'm sorry," Nancy said. "But it will be all right if I run in once in a while won't it? I'd like to talk to you about several things."

"Come ahead."

After she hung up, Nancy sat lost in thought. No mystery she had ever tried to solve had baffled her more than this one. In addition, George Fayne had not recovered from her frightening experience.

"I feel simply terrible about it," Nancy told Hannah Gruen. "George is weak and has no appetite. But what's even worse, she mopes around talking about the party thieves and begging me to give up the case every time I see her."

"They've had a doctor for her?"

"Yes."

"What does he say?"

"That George's trouble is mostly mental."

"For all we know those dreadful criminals may have threatened her in some way," Hannah suggested.

"It would explain her pleas to me to drop the case," Nancy conceded.

As she left the house, Nancy mulled over Hannah's idea. She was on her way to see Mr. Lightner about Linda but decided to stop at George's home first. There was the same old story again but with a new twist this time. George said that she had had a dream which she knew was a premonition and warning.

"Nancy, you were being dropped over a cliff by a man in a velvet mask," the distraught girl said. "That's something you can't laugh off."

"I'll avoid all cliffs," Nancy humored her.

Ordinarily George would have smiled, but now she remained serious and did not make her usual witty comeback. Nor could she be coaxed out of her low state of mind. Nancy's parting "Cheer up, pal!" met with a blank response.

"Something must be done about George!" Nancy told herself as she hurried on to the Lightner office. "If I solve the mystery, that may do it."

She went at once to Mr. Lightner's office. He

listened politely to her request that he take Linda back but shook his head.

"In the main I leave employment matters in that department entirely to Mr. Tombar," he said. "If he discharged Linda, there must have been a good reason. Besides, the girl has been under suspicion."

"Unjustly so, I'm sure, Mr. Lightner. She wasn't even at that musicale where there was a robbery."

"I know," Mr. Lightner said. "But there were other parties and certain thefts right here which raised doubts as to her honesty."

"If I could prove she's innocent, would you take Linda back?" Nancy asked.

"Why—uh—yes. Of course—that is, with Tombar's okay."

Nancy realized that Linda would need a reference to secure a new job. She could not get one from her former employer.

Nancy thought quickly. Could she help Linda another way? This might be Nancy's chance to get an invitation to the affair on June twenty-sixth. If only she could catch any of the thieves who might show up!

"Mr. Lightner," she said, "you know by this time that I've been trying to help Dad solve the mystery of the party thieves."

He smiled. "Yes. He told me even I was under suspicion for a time!"

Nancy blushed and changed the subject. "May I go to the lecture at the Claytons'?" she asked.

He readily gave his consent, telling her to meet him there at seven thirty that evening.

"I'm taking personal charge," he informed her. "I've decided it's high time I did a little investigating of my own."

"Then Mr. Tombar won't be there?" Nancy asked.

"No," Mr. Lightner replied. "He's in a huff about it, too. But that's beside the point."

Further conversation revealed that Peter Tombar was annoyed also because Mr. Lightner had asked him not to take such long lunch hours.

Nancy smiled. "The man must have been driving out into the country a good deal," she thought. "Well, if he doesn't go any more, that clue's washed out for me."

Speaking again of the lecture, she suggested that as a precautionary measure all the cards of admission to be sent to the people who accepted be marked with a special swirl. Then no uninvited person could possibly get in without being detected. Mr. Lightner immediately agreed to Nancy's proposal.

"I have the list here, ready for addressing," he told her. "Shall we mark them now?"

The work was done quickly. Each card was marked on the reverse side with ink, in such a manner that the identifying character could not be altered without giving evidence of it.

"It's essential that we tell no one what we've done," Nancy advised Mr. Lightner. "Not even your secretary or Mr. Tombar."

"Surely both of them can be trusted."

"Nevertheless, let's keep this our own secret."

"Very well," Mr. Lightner said. "I'll personally check every invitation at the door. In that way we'll make certain no one who shouldn't be there gets past us."

While waiting for the twenty-sixth, Nancy went to Mr. Johnson's office to inquire what progress had been made in recalling the charge plates. She learned that they were coming in very slowly. He said that he did not dare push the matter, lest any dishonest employee gain an inkling of what lay behind the scheme.

"I'll let you know if anything turns up," the credit manager promised. "But I doubt that it will."

Nancy had a long talk with her father. He said that he had decided to take the Lightner case, thanks to his daughter's fine sleuthing. But the company owner refused to believe that any of his employees were not honest.

"His clients are getting a bit impatient to start their suits," the lawyer revealed, "but we're stalling for time."

"If I could only uncover something worth

while!" Nancy sighed. "If you hadn't been such a good teacher, Dad, I'd certainly go to the police and insist that they shadow Tombar."

"Well, I'm glad you're using your head, Nancy," Mr. Drew said. "You have nothing concrete to base your suspicions on as yet."

"I know it."

"But your hunches are usually good, my dear, so keep after him."

Nancy said indeed she would, but spent most of Wednesday with George who had sent for her. The distraught girl begged again that Nancy give up the case.

"I'll be careful, really I will," Nancy promised. "Tomorrow I'm going to a perfectly safe high-brow lecture!"

George was in no better spirits and Nancy missed her help. All she could do was humor her. Bess was out of town, leaving Nancy with a lonesome feeling.

"But I mustn't give up, even for a second," she determined.

The next evening Nancy arrived at the Clayton home early. It had been a gloomy, dark day and all the lights in the house were on. To her chagrin she found not only Mr. Lightner there, but also his assistant, Mr. Tombar.

"It wasn't necessary for him to be here," Mr. Lightner admitted to Nancy. "But he insisted. Said he felt I might run into difficulty in handling some of the details I wasn't used to. Of course, this is Mr. Tombar's usual work—"

Nancy smiled and made no comment. It was obvious to her that Mr. Tombar wanted to be there! Making a great show of directing the placement of chairs, he bustled about, growling orders at everyone.

"No! No!" he yelled as a maid moved a row to make more aisle space. "Leave the chairs as I've placed them!"

Nancy was disgusted with his rudeness. The maid was employed by the Claytons, not the entertainment company. Tombar must have guessed her thoughts. Angrily he turned on her.

"You're always underfoot!" he cried out, his eyes flashing. "If you'd tend to your own affairs, we could work better."

Nancy flushed but made no response. She went to find Mr. Lightner.

He had posted himself at the front door to inspect each card that was presented. Nancy stood close by to scrutinize the people as they passed. Everyone was straightforward-looking and above suspicion.

"So far, so good," Mr. Lightner presently whispered to the girl. "At least two thirds of the cards are in. All are authentic."

Nancy had observed a man loitering outdoors near the parking lot. She called Mr. Lightner's attention to him.

"Oh, don't worry about him," she was told. "He's a private detective I employed. After the lecture starts, he'll move inside and help keep an eye on the guests."

In a few minutes the lecture began. Not all the cards had been turned in, so Mr. Lightner remained at the front door to meet latecomers.

"It looks as if the masked thief and his cohorts aren't going to show up," Nancy remarked. "Just to be sure no one's prowling about the grounds, though, I'll walk around outside and see if there's anyone suspicious."

She circled the house, noting that all the windows on the first floor were very high from the ground. It would be difficult to climb in and dangerous to drop from any of them!

In her tour Nancy presently came to the parking area and wandered among the cars. A lookout might be stationed in one of them! As she approached a long black sedan, Nancy was startled to see a man lying on the ground, almost under the front wheels.

"Oh," she thought, "he's ill!" and rushed to his side.

Kneeling, she realized that he had been knocked unconscious.

As wild ideas raced through Nancy's mind, she received a further shock. All the lights in the Clayton house suddenly went out!

CHAPTER XIV

Loot for Sale

IT WOULD be cruel to leave the man who lay unconscious on the ground. Yet Nancy wanted to return to the suddenly darkened house. She was sure another robbery was in progress!

As she sought to revive the stranger, she noticed a sweet-smelling but peculiar odor on his clothing. Instantly she thought of George's experience on the train. This man's assailant had done a good job of knocking him out. First a blow on the head, as evidenced by some swelling, then drugged.

Repeatedly, Nancy called out "Stop thief!" to warn those inside the house. She wondered if anyone inside could hear her. Minutes later the lights went on again.

"If only someone would come here so I could leave!" Nancy thought unhappily. "The thieves are probably making a getaway this very minute."

Vainly she hoped that members of the Velvet Gang would try to escape through the parking area, thus giving her a chance to intercept them. But time passed and no one came that way.

Nancy chafed the stranger's wrists, slapped him gently on the cheek, and finally he began to revive. He stared blankly into her face and mumbled:

"Where am I? What happened?"

"You're by your car at the Claytons'," Nancy told him. She helped the man sit up. "Can you recall what happened?" she asked.

"It's coming back now," he muttered, brushing a hand across his eyes. "As I got out of the car I was knocked on the head. That's the last I remember."

"Your wallet. Do you still have it?"

The guest fumbled in his pocket. "Gone," he admitted ruefully. "I've been robbed."

"Did it contain anything besides money?" Nancy asked.

"Yes—several cards, including the one to the lecture."

The man identified himself as Albert G. Brunner and said he had come alone. Nancy introduced herself and told him of her suspicions.

"So you're the young detective I read about every so often," he said.

Nancy acknowledged that she was and offered

to help Mr. Brunner into the house where a doctor could be summoned.

"By leaning on me do you think you can make it?" she asked anxiously.

"I'll try," the man replied. "Once on my feet, I should be okay. I've been drugged all right. I remember now that just as I fell a handkerchief with a peculiar odor on it was pressed to my nose."

Nancy managed to assist him the short distance to the house. There she was relieved of his care by two solicitous servants, who did not seem upset by anything that might have happened in the house. Nancy began to wonder if she was wrong about the thieves.

Instantly she sought Mr. Lightner and told him of her suspicions. Even he had believed the darkness a temporary power shutoff.

An investigation was started at once. It revealed that valuable silver pieces and figurines were missing from the first floor and jewelry from the second.

"This will ruin me!" Mr. Lightner confided to Nancy. "I'll have to go out of business! What'll I do?" He walked back and forth excitedly.

"Surely it isn't that bad," Nancy said kindly. "By the way, where is Mr. Tombar?"

"I haven't seen him. I suppose he's out looking for those thieves."

Nancy decided to find out for herself. Hurry-

ing from room to room, she finally located him in
the kitchen, lecturing his caterers for being so
slow.

"Guests aren't going to stand around all night
waiting to be served!" he stormed.

Nancy watched Mr. Tombar until he was free,
then nonchalantly started talking to him about
the theft.

"I was outdoors and didn't see a thing," she
said chattily. "But I'd have been terribly scared.
Weren't you?"

"No."

"Was that because you didn't see anything?"

"Say, what is this, a third degree?" Tombar
snapped at her. "I haven't got time to talk." He
stalked off.

There was nothing more she could do. The
police had arrived and taken charge. Nancy
listened as they made the usual checkup. The
same robbery pattern as used before. Not a clue
left by the wily party thieves!

On the way home Nancy thought about the
Velvet Gang. They would never be caught by
ordinary methods. They were too cunning and
clever at anticipating traps laid for them.

Nancy's thoughts also turned to Tombar. The
man was an enigma. He was certainly faithful
to his job, yet his behavior was so unspeakable
that it made him seem suspicious. Since he had
had nothing to do with the marked invitations,

however, her former doubts on that score could be eliminated.

"Still I don't trust him," Nancy told herself. "I wish I could go to that wedding Saturday night. Then I could watch Tombar myself. But I can't send regrets to Helen Tyne's dance at this late date. And Ned would never forgive me if I disappointed him."

Next morning at breakfast Nancy was turning over several plans of action in her mind when Bess Marvin arrived.

"Hi, Nancy!" she said but did not smile.

"Hello, yourself. What's wrong, Bess? You don't usually get over here so early."

"It's George. She's in bed again, Nancy. The doctor says she's still suffering from the effects of that frightening kidnaping episode. Personally, I think it's more than that. George is scared out of her wits about something."

"She never was frightened of anything before."

"I know," Bess admitted soberly. "I always was the timid one of our trio. Something strange has come over her—it's as if she were under a spell. Won't you talk to her? For some reason, she's especially troubled about you."

"Me?" Nancy echoed as they left the house at once to call on George.

The girl did not look ill, propped up against the pillows with a tray of food in front of her. After

Nancy had chatted with her a few minutes, however, she knew that Bess was right.

"What happened last night?" George asked anxiously. "I read about the robbery in the paper. I'm sure you were there."

"Yes."

"Nancy, I asked you to give up the case!" George cried out hysterically. "You don't understand what you're up against. Those awful people will stop at nothing—nothing—"

Bess and Nancy soothed their friend as best they could, but Nancy would not promise to give up her sleuthing completely. Mrs. Fayne came in to attend her daughter, and a few minutes afterward the girls left.

"Just seeing me seems to excite poor George," Nancy remarked as she and Bess reached the sidewalk.

"We must avoid talking about the case when we're with her," Bess suggested.

"But she's the one who always brings it up," Nancy said with a sigh. "Bess, this is awful. It's like losing the best pal we have."

"I know it. Maybe you ought to give up the case—or at least pretend to. Then maybe George will get better."

"I'll follow your advice," Nancy promised. "I'll do a good pretending job. Right now, I'm going to Taylor's. Want to come along?"

"Sure. Only I haven't much money." Bess giggled.

Nancy bought an apron for Hannah Gruen, then they called on Mr. Johnson to ask about the return of charge plates.

"Not many have come in," he reported. "We're too busy to go around collecting them. Sorry. I'll let you know what happens."

Nancy was deeply disappointed by his lack of interest. "I can't understand it," she told Bess as they went downstairs. "He doesn't seem to care whether he has a thief working for him or not."

As they passed the jewelry counter, Nancy caught sight of Alice Thompson, a former classmate, who had recently taken a job at Taylor's. The three girls chatted for a few minutes. Then, with deliberate intent, Nancy asked the girl if she had turned in her charge plate as requested by the management.

"Why, no," Alice replied. "I was going to, but then a note came around changing the order."

"Changing it! Why?"

"I don't know. It just said we weren't to turn the plates in after all."

"So that's why so few were returned," Nancy mused. "I wonder if Mr. Johnson himself sent out the order?"

Curious to learn the truth, she and Bess immediately returned to the credit manager's office. Mr. Johnson was elsewhere in the store, but his secretary assured the girls that the order had not come from him.

"If I were you, though, I wouldn't bother him about it," she advised. "He has an important conference today. The entire matter is annoying to him."

Nancy already knew this. She felt completely frustrated. Such a good clue just being thrown away!

"I guess I'll have to give up the idea," she admitted to Bess.

"Oh, you'll think up some other scheme," her friend said loyally.

With time on their hands, the girls idled through the store. Bess looked at blouses and selected one to be held until she received her allowance. Finally they returned to the jewelry department to find a birthday present for Mrs. Marvin.

"A new assortment of art objects just came in this morning," Alice told Bess. "We have a lovely miniature painted on porcelain. I'll show it to you."

"I'm afraid that would be too expensive—"

"Not this one." Alice smiled. "The price, in my opinion, is ridiculously low. In fact, I was amazed when I saw the tag. Do let me show it to you."

She led the girls to a counter on which were displayed a number of small gifts. One of them was a miniature of Marie Antoinette.

Nancy drew in her breath, stunned. The lovely picture looked exactly like the one which had been stolen from Gloria Hendrick's home!

"This can't be the same!" she gasped. "It must be a copy—and yet it doesn't look like a copy. The gold frame has a number of tiny scratches on it as if it were old.

"Bess, I'm sure this was stolen from the Hendricks!"

CHAPTER XV

An Investigation

GREATLY excited by Nancy's discovery, Alice asked her how she knew that the miniature was stolen. Bess and Nancy examined it in minute detail, and told of having seen the miniature before the robbery.

"But Taylor's wouldn't accept stolen merchandise, Nancy," the young clerk objected.

"Not knowingly. But this may have been sold to them without their realizing it was stolen. Perhaps they got it from an antique dealer."

All agreed that the miniature was greatly underpriced, even if it were only an excellent copy of the original.

Nancy promptly bought the miniature. She would find out for certain if it had been stolen from the Hendricks.

"Have you others like these?" Nancy asked Alice.

"I know a shipment came in, but all the merchandise isn't on the floor yet," the girl replied. "I'll ask Mr. Watkins about it. He's head of our department."

Mr. Watkins was a stubby, white-haired old man with glasses. When he saw the miniature which was being wrapped for Nancy, he glanced quickly at the tag.

"This item must have been mismarked," he said. "Taylor's wouldn't ask to have it back, of course, but I must check invoices before any more articles in the shipment are sold."

Nancy expressed a desire to see the other miniatures immediately, if they were for sale.

"We'll look into this," the elderly clerk said. "Come with me to the marking room."

He led the girls to a rear exit and across a dark alleyway to a building used for receiving and marking.

"Snecker!" he called loudly, switching on an overhead light. "Hey, Snecker! Where is he?" Mr. Watkins asked as a young clerk emerged from an adjoining room.

"He's not here," the boy said. "Mr. Snecker's taken the day off."

"Again?" Mr. Watkins remarked irritably.

To Nancy and Bess he explained that Burt Snecker was in charge of uncrating and marking all items to be put on sale and shipping damaged goods back to factories. Nancy was interested.

Next morning Nancy hurried to the department store. To her disappointment, Mr. Snecker had telephoned that he was too ill to work.

"Very likely he's out fishing," Mr. Watkins grumbled. "That young clerk of his can't do all the work. Things are getting behind."

During the brief conversation with the elderly man, Nancy managed to get two valuable bits of information from him.

First she learned that the note sent to employees countermanding the order to turn in their charge plates had been unsigned. At once Nancy became suspicious and her thoughts turned to Snecker and the stolen miniature.

"Do you know where Mr. Snecker lives?" she asked Mr. Watkins.

"I can tell you in a minute." He consulted a book under the counter. "He lives at twenty-four Tanner Street. You goin' to see him?" A look of amusement crossed the elderly man's face and he shook his head. "When women get their hearts set on a thing, they sure go after it. Well, I hope Snecker can tell you what you want to know about the Marie Antoinette miniature."

Nancy smiled, thanked Mr. Watkins for the information, and left the store.

"At least," she thought determinedly as she went to her car, "I'll try to find out something from Mr. Snecker before Mrs. Hendrick turns this matter over to the police."

She stopped to ask the way from a traffic officer. He gave directions to a section of River Heights with which she was not familiar.

"Tanner Street," she mused. "Must be in an old section of town."

Nancy was right. The vicinity in which the apartment house was located was poor and densely settled. She was obliged to drive very slowly, as the streets were filled with children playing.

After riding through several drab, unattractive streets, Nancy finally came to the one she sought. The house where the Sneckers lived was at the far end of it. The red-brick dwelling, composed of four stories, was run-down and outmoded.

She applied her brakes, intending to pull into a vacant space a short distance beyond the building. As she slowed down, another car which had been parked directly in front of the house pulled away from the curb.

"Now, where have I seen that car before?" Nancy thought.

Her pulse quickened. The car was a mud-splattered green sedan. Though she caught only a fleeting glimpse of the driver, she recognized him at once.

"That's Peter Tombar!" she thought. "Could he have been visiting Burt Snecker? And why?"

CHAPTER XVI

A Discovery

NANCY wanted to follow Tombar. She might pick up a clue that would help piece the puzzle together.

But almost at once she discarded the idea in favor of calling on the Sneckers. She had an excuse which she could not use another time—an excuse which might prove helpful in solving the mystery.

Nancy noted Tombar's license number, however, then parked at the curb and went into the apartment-house vestibule. Looking at the letter boxes, she pressed a buzzer above the name of Burt Snecker. In a moment a shrill feminine voice answered through the tube:

"Who's there?"

"I'm from Taylor's," Nancy replied, purposely not giving her name.

"Oh, a salesgirl!" the woman exclaimed. She

129

seemed a trifle flustered. "I'll be right down."

"May I come up?"

"Just a minute. I'll be with you," the woman said, ignoring the request.

Nancy waited in the stuffy vestibule. She could not step inside the hall, for Mrs. Snecker had not unlocked the door.

In a moment she appeared, breathing heavily from her haste. She was a tall woman, with a determined chin and narrow blue eyes.

"You are Mrs. Snecker?" Nancy asked to make certain of her identification.

"That's my name." The woman eyed her warily. "The store sent you, you said?"

"I came to inquire about your husband. We're concerned because of his absence."

"Burt is sick again."

"I'm sorry to hear that. Nothing serious, I hope."

"He's in bed with the asthma. I tell 'im if he'd stay away from the river he wouldn't get these attacks. He's supposed to take some medicine, but how can he when we don't have no money?"

"You're having a hard time of it?" Nancy feigned concern.

"Whadda you expect on his salary? Maybe he ain't no hustler, if you know what I mean. I tell 'im he ought to ask for more, but—"

Mrs. Snecker's tirade was interrupted by a loud call from up the stairway.

"Florence! Florence! Come here, will you?"

"That's him callin' me now," Mrs. Snecker said. "He's a nuisance when he's sick. Always keepin' me on the run. He wants me to wait on 'im like he was a baby."

Nancy could see that the woman was completely out of sorts.

"You needn't tell the store what I just said," Mrs. Snecker advised hastily. "I shouldn't 'a' spoke my piece, but Burt's got me down with his gripes and complaints. When he works, things ain't so bad. Oh, well, we'll soon be out of these shabby quarters."

"You're moving to a better apartment?"

"You bet we are."

"But I thought you just said Mr. Snecker's salary isn't large and he's not a go-getter."

"Not at store business, he ain't. But he's got another line he's working." Mrs. Snecker dropped her voice, so that it could not possibly carry upstairs. "We'll soon be on easy street, struttin' with the best of 'em!"

"Like your friends the Tombars?" Nancy asked.

"Sure, and believe me—"

Mrs. Snecker suddenly broke off, staring suspiciously at the girl. Belatedly, it dawned upon her that she had talked too freely.

Without another word, she slammed the door shut and disappeared up the stairway. Nancy tried to get in, for she wanted to talk to Mr. Snecker, but unfortunately the door had locked automatically.

"Oh, well," she thought, returning to her car, "I learned something. The Sneckers and the Tombars are friends!"

As she drove through the downtown section of River Heights, Nancy also reflected on the remark that the woman had made about Snecker's other work that would "put them on easy street." Did it include Tombar?

On Monday morning, while passing the offices of the Lightner Entertainment Company, Nancy decided to drop in and see Mr. Lightner. He had just finished dictating a letter and welcomed the opportunity to chat with the girl detective. He was in better spirits than when she had seen him before.

"The wedding last Saturday, Miss Drew, went off like clockwork. No thefts or even attempted ones," he told her.

Nancy said that she was pleased to hear this.

"But it doesn't prove that the thieves have ceased their activities," she said. "They know the police are hard on their trail, especially after George's experience. So they may have decided to lay low for a while."

"True." The company official sighed. "Well, let's hope for the best. I certainly will keep pressing the police. I want to recover my own stolen costumes and masks."

Masks was a favorite subject with Mr. Lightner. At once he began to talk about them. He told Nancy of his extensive trips through America, Europe, and Asia to assemble his fine collection. He had turned over several Egyptian and Roman death masks to the local museum.

"Those were the masks placed over the faces of deceased persons or mummies, weren't they?" Nancy asked.

"That's right," Mr. Lightner nodded. "Often a mask was made for a person while he was still alive. In this way it was so realistic that today we know about various types of ancient people from them."

Mr. Lightner would have talked on at length, but Nancy had other business. When a pause came in the conversation, she said:

"Linda Seeley knew a great deal about masks, and in fact all your work, didn't she?" As the man nodded, Nancy remarked, "I should think you'd miss her very much."

"Well, yes, we do."

"Then why not take her back?" Nancy suggested.

Mr. Lightner frowned. "You'll have to discuss that with Mr. Tombar," he said. "I can't interfere. He handles all such matters."

"But have I your permission to talk to him about her?"

"Certainly. Go ahead. I don't think you'll get very far, though."

Nancy shared the same opinion. Nevertheless, she felt that it would not do any harm to talk with Tombar about Linda. Accordingly, she sought him back in the costume rooms.

"He's busy and I have no idea how long he'll be tied up," a stenographer informed her.

"That's all right. I'll wait."

Tombar was talking loudly. Nancy, seated in a chair near the door, could not help overhearing his angry voice.

"No, I won't do it!" Tombar exclaimed. "Quit trying to persuade me. I wish you wouldn't keep pestering me. I've told you before never to bother me when I'm on the job. This time I mean it."

His visitor's reply was so soft spoken that Nancy could not catch the words.

But Mr. Tombar's next outburst was fairly shouted. "Get out of here, Harris!" he roared. "Get out before I throw you out!"

Nancy expected the two men to come to blows. She was sure that Tombar would stop at nothing to get rid of his annoying visitor.

Just then the door was flung open and Mr. Harris rushed out so fast that Nancy did not get a clear view of his face. She was confronted by

Mr. Tombar. He was so enraged that his red face looked as if he might burst a blood vessel at any moment.

He sprang toward her, shaking his fist in front of her bewildered face.

"You here again!" he exclaimed. "You little eavesdropper! Spying on me! Well, I won't have it!"

CHAPTER XVII

Blue Iris Inn

THOUGH furious at Mr. Tombar's outburst, Nancy gave no indication of her feeling.

"Spying?" she echoed. "I'm sure I don't know what you mean."

"You young nuisance!" Tombar snapped. "You're always around!"

Nancy smiled and remained silent.

"Well, since you're so curious," the man said, "I'll tell you why Mr. Richard Harris was here. He's trying to sell me a cemetery plot, and I don't want to buy it. That's all."

Nancy was certain that the man was lying, but she pretended to accept his explanation.

"It's not pleasant to think about dying," she said, "but I suppose it's necessary."

"Hm—yes. Well, what else do you want to know?" Mr. Tombar became a trifle more agreeable.

Nancy told him of the purpose of her call—to ask that he take Linda Seeley back.

"I'm sure she's innocent and won't cause you any trouble."

"Nothing doing," Mr. Tombar replied shortly. "I don't trust her."

Nancy outlined several sound reasons why the girl should be rehired, but the man gazed at her coldly. It was plain that he could not be swayed.

"I have someone else in mind," he stated.

The telephone rang, and Mr. Tombar stepped to his desk to answer it. Though he lowered his voice, Nancy heard him speak the name Florence. Instantly her suspicions were aroused. Was he talking to Florence Snecker? What business might they have together?

Try as she would, Nancy could not figure out anything about the call because the conversation was one-sided, the other person doing all the talking. Finally slamming down the receiver and turning almost purple with rage, Mr. Tombar glared at Nancy in the doorway.

"I knew it! Trying to get an earful again!" he screamed. "Well, this is the last time!"

Fists clenched, he started toward Nancy as if intending to harm her. Midway across the room he stopped in dismay, staring over her shoulder.

Nancy turned. Directly behind her stood Mr. Lightner, glowering at his employee.

"What's going on here?" he demanded.

"Why, I—that is—Miss Drew is always interfering—" Mr. Tombar stammered.

"That's no excuse for your actions, Tombar. You'd better explain further."

"I—I'm sorry, Mr. Lightner. My apology. I didn't mean any harm. I—I—"

Nancy escaped to the hall so that the two men might talk privately. But they did not close the door, and as she paused to get a drink at a water cooler, she could hear them plainly.

"Tombar, I've given you free rein in the business since you asked me a few months ago," Mr. Lightner said icily. "I permitted you to take complete charge in this department. Without my knowledge you discharged Miss Seeley, though personally I liked her work.

"And since then matters in this department have been no better—if anything, they're worse. Records in bad shape. Customers dissatisfied.

"And now I hear you threatening Miss Drew, who happens to be the daughter of one of my very good friends. This is the last straw."

"I gave an apology."

"It is accepted," Mr. Lightner returned. "And also your resignation."

"My resignation! You're not firing me! You can't do that. I've been here four years and people depend on me—"

"I can and I have," the president corrected.

"Pick up your pay check as you leave. I think there is nothing more to discuss."

Mr. Lightner turned on his heel and left the office. Meeting Nancy in the hall he assured her that she was welcome to return at any time, and he was sorry for what had happened.

"I know it wasn't your fault," he said.

The president promised that he would look into Linda's case as soon as he had a spare moment. Nancy thanked him and started for the door.

At this moment she saw Tombar stride out of the building by a side entrance. He had not waited for his pay check!

"That will give him an excuse to come back here later, if he wants to," she thought, and left the building.

Her next stop was her father's office. Through him she learned that Mr. Harris, instead of being a cemetery association salesman, was connected with a downtown real-estate firm.

"I'm afraid Tombar is doing a lot of covering up," the lawyer stated.

"Covering up shady deals," Nancy declared.

"Maybe I should have him followed," Mr. Drew suggested.

"If he found out about it, we might never learn what we suspect," Nancy said. "Give me a little longer, Dad. At least until you've finished the brief you're working on."

"Well, all right," her father said.

Obtaining Mr. Harris' address, Nancy went to his office on White Avenue. She told him quite frankly that the purpose of her call was to learn of his business connection with Mr. Tombar. Still irritated by the treatment he had received, the agent willingly answered her query.

"I asked Mr. Tombar to sell the old Blue Iris Inn," he disclosed. "Do you know the place?"

Nancy shook her head. "No. I never heard of it."

"It's a picturesque old inn out in the country on Woodland Road. An isolated place and in run-down condition. All the same, it could be converted into a top-notch dine and dance spot.

"I have a client who wants to develop the property. Tombar bought the place for a song and could make a neat profit on it."

"He doesn't want to sell?"

"We offered him double what he paid for it. He won't even discuss the matter."

"Maybe he plans to develop the place himself."

"Tombar?" Mr. Harris smiled. "I doubt it. He's just stubborn, that's all."

Nancy was sure that there was more than stubbornness back of the refusal. She asked the real-estate agent for a description of the old inn. He told her that it was a clapboard structure, situated about eighteen miles from River Heights.

"I'll bet that's where Mr. Tombar used to go on his lunch hour," Nancy reflected. "He'd just about have time to make it in two hours, if he drove fast and didn't stay too long."

Recalling the muddy tires on Tombar's car, she asked Mr. Harris if Woodland Road were paved.

"Not all the way. That's one of the bad features," the agent admitted. "My client can finance the paving, though, for the short distance that would be necessary. If you have influence with Tombar, I wish you'd advise him to sell the inn. Since it is fast falling into ruin, he would be fortunate indeed to get rid of it now."

"I'm afraid I wouldn't have much luck in persuading Mr. Tombar to sell it, either," Nancy replied.

The name of the old Blue Iris Inn intrigued Nancy. She would have enjoyed looking it over under any circumstances. Now, knowing its owner was Peter Tombar, she had a particular desire to see it. Nancy did some marketing for Mrs. Gruen, picked up her car, and wondered what her next move should be.

Reaching home, she telephoned Bess Marvin at once, bringing her up to date on what had happened and inviting her to drive out to the Blue Iris Inn early the next morning.

"Just the two of us? Alone?" Bess asked dubiously.

"Why, yes. Unless George can go. There's no chance of that, I suppose?"

"Don't even let her know you're making the trip," Bess advised hastily. "I was over there a little while ago. She's out of bed, but not herself at all. Her family is terribly worried about her. Isn't it awful, Nancy? By the way, she spent most of the time talking about you."

"Again?"

"She's so afraid you'll get hurt by the Velvet Gang."

"I wish she could forget that worry."

"She's obsessed by it. So whatever you do, don't mention the Blue Iris Inn to her."

"I won't," Nancy promised, deeply concerned.

"You'll go with me, though?"

"I suppose so," Bess consented reluctantly. "I hate to do it, but I won't let you down. When shall we start?"

"Right after breakfast. I'll stop by for you at nine o'clock." Nancy laughed, and added with a chuckle, "Better pack some sandwiches and a thermos of milk, too! The dining room won't be open at Blue Iris Inn. And I have a hunch we may spend a long day there!"

"Oh, Nancy, in that spooky, closed-up place. The very thought of it gives me the shivers!"

CHAPTER XVIII

Nancy's Disguise

THE SUN blazed overhead next morning when Nancy and Bess finally came within view of the rambling old Blue Iris Inn.

Far removed from surrounding farmhouses, the wooden building stood lonely and forlorn in a spot shaded by tall pines. Flower beds, including the iris from which the inn had taken its name, were choked with weeds.

Parking some distance from the inn, Nancy and Bess advanced cautiously in case Mr. Tombar should be around. Their attention was focused on the windows, all of which were boarded up.

"This place gives me the creeps," Bess said. "I wouldn't want to have even a picnic here."

Nancy laughed. "It really could be fixed up quite attractively."

The girls circled the inn, peering through chinks in the boards which covered the windows.

To their amazement, they could see in the dim interior that most of the rooms on the lower floor were cluttered with boxes and crates, many of them with lids apparently tightly fastened.

"Looks like a warehouse," Bess remarked.

"Or a department store shipping room," Nancy added.

They speculated on whether the boxes had been brought to the inn for unpacking, or had been filled there and were ready for shipment.

"I wonder if these boxes came from Taylor's," Nancy said. "Snecker works in the receiving and marking room. And he's a friend of Tombar."

"Do you think they may contain stolen goods?"

"It looks that way, Bess. I wish we could get inside the inn and open up one of those cases."

"We might be caught," Bess shivered.

Nancy made a careful inspection of the windows, and tested every door. She quickly reached the conclusion that the inn had been effectively barricaded.

"We can't get in without smashing some of the boards," she decided. "And that might land us in jail."

"Let's return to town and notify the police, Nancy."

"I guess we'll have to," Nancy sighed. "But I'd like to find a way inside. You know, Bess, this Chinese puzzle we've been working on is beginning to take a definite form."

"Not for me it isn't."

"Remember the charge plate that I found on the railroad track?"

"Of course."

"Well, it must have belonged to Snecker. Now, unless those boxes and cartons contain Blue Iris furnishings, I'm convinced there's something strange about their being here."

"I think so too, Nancy. But if it should turn out that they're filled with goods from the inn, wouldn't we look silly reporting it to the police?"

"Before I tell them, I'll do a little more checking," Nancy agreed. "Come on, Bess! We've learned everything we can here. Let's get back to town. I want to find out about those boxes if I can."

In River Heights once more, the girls had lunch, then Nancy went straight to her father. Through people he contacted she learned that at the time the Blue Iris Inn was sold, all the furnishings had been disposed of at auction. She asked his advice about telling the police her suspicions.

"Well, actually you haven't much to go on," he said. "Better do a little more investigating first. For instance, find out, if you can, whether Tombar himself bought some of the furnishings at the auction."

Nancy set off for the office of the auctioneer. A short distance from it she met Mr. Lightner.

"I'm glad I ran into you, Miss Drew!" he declared cordially. "I've been trying to reach you by telephone all morning."

"I've been for a ride in the country."

"I was afraid you might have forgotten the day," he reminded her.

"It's July first."

"And the third date listed on the lining of the velvet hood. Linda Seeley told me about your suspicions. I'd like you to attend the party if you can. It's a dance at the John Dwight estate. At the last minute they decided to make it a masquerade."

"I'd like to go."

"I'll arrange for a costume," he offered. "How would you like to dress? As a French lady or another Spanish señorita?"

"As a sleuth." Nancy laughed. "How about my being a maid in the women's cloakroom?"

"Why, yes. A splendid place for scrutinizing guests. Come with me now and I'll find an outfit for you."

Nancy decided to postpone her call to the auctioneer's office. At the entertainment company she selected a well-tailored black dress with white collar and cuffs and a dainty ruffled cap.

"I have some news for you," Mr. Lightner said, walking with Nancy to the front door. "I'm taking Linda Seeley back."

"Oh, I'm so glad!"

To have Linda reinstated in the firm was a great relief to Nancy. Nevertheless, she knew that Mr. Lightner had re-employed the girl largely on her recommendation. Should the thefts which had damaged the company's reputation continue, Linda might be blamed again.

"That makes this party tonight an important one," Nancy thought. "Oh, I do hope everything goes off without trouble!"

Arriving home with her big box, Nancy was pleasantly surprised to find Ned Nickerson lounging on the porch.

"Schoolbooks are locked up," he joked. Seizing Nancy, he planted a kiss on her cheek. "You look wonderful!"

"Ned! The neighbors!" Nancy blushed. "But I'm glad to see you."

"What's in the box? A new dress for a date with me tonight?"

"Maybe."

Nancy told him of her plan to play the part of a maid at the Dwight party.

"How about coming with me? I think I could get you in as a hat-check boy or something of the sort. Want to help me catch a couple of masked thieves?"

"Wel-l," Ned weakened, "since you put it that way, the answer is, naturally, yes. But what do I know about checking men's hats or coats?"

"It's easy, and maybe you'll spot one of the

Velvet Gang. Come inside, and I'll telephone Mr. Lightner."

Arrangements were made for Ned to obtain suitable clothing and assist the regular checker from Lightner's.

"Now bring me up to date on what's happened," Ned urged Nancy. "Remember, I've been buried in exams since I last saw you."

Rapidly she related how the continuing thefts had threatened Mr. Lightner's company with ruin. She told him about Peter Tombar and Burt Snecker, and their apparent association.

"I'm inclined to think that both of them are mixed up in the thefts," she concluded. "The Velvet Gang may be working with them. At any rate, I'm investigating the Blue Iris Inn next."

"I'm surprised that you and George haven't been out there tearing the place apart board by board," Ned remarked, grinning.

At mention of George, Nancy sobered and informed him of George's unhappy state of mind.

"Her parents are worried and so am I," she said. "We can't understand what's wrong."

"I'm sorry to hear that," Ned said. "George is such a good scout."

He went home to dinner but was back at the Drews' by seven o'clock.

"You're a very handsome checkroom boy!" Nancy declared when she saw him in his uniform. "How do I look?"

"Lovely, but not natural. What a hair-do!"

"I had to disguise myself as much as I could."

Over her arm she carried an old loose fitting coat of Hannah's and a large hat that could be pulled down low on her head.

"These are just in case—" Nancy laughed.

"Be careful tonight, both of you," Mr. Drew warned as the couple left the house. "I'll wait up until you're safely home."

Mr. Lightner, who had arrived early, was waiting for Nancy. He whispered that every precaution had been taken to avert another robbery and no trouble was expected.

"Six plain-clothes men are here to watch the guests. Nothing can go wrong."

Nancy and Ned were assigned to separate cloakrooms upstairs. Nancy found herself paired with a rather indifferent maid named Hilda.

"All we have to do is stay here and help the ladies with their things," the girl told Nancy. "Just don't get the coats mixed up, that's all."

For the next hour Nancy checked guests' belongings efficiently, and quickly hung them on racks. Many of the costumes worn were very lovely and she recognized some as having been rented from Lightner's.

Masks were of every form and shape. The small black half-masks were by far the most popular, due probably to the warm night. Nancy could not recognize anyone.

"A mask really can change one's appearance completely," she remarked to Hilda during a lull in their work. "Did you know that George Washington ordered a velvet mask for his six-year-old stepdaughter and wife to wear on the street so they would not be recognized?"

"I didn't know Washington had a stepdaughter," Hilda said indifferently.

"Oh, yes. And fashionable ladies in Colonial days wore masks to protect their make-up from the sun and rain."

"Yeah?" Hilda regarded Nancy with sudden suspicion. "Say, you do a lot of reading, don't you. Been a maid long?"

"Only a short while."

"You got a lot to learn," Hilda told her. "You better quit mooning about masks and remember where you put things. When the women start comin' for their coats, they'll want 'em fast."

"I'll not let you down," Nancy promised.

She said no more about masks and devoted herself strictly to her duties as maid. After the dancing had started in the ballroom below, Mr. Lightner came upstairs. He informed Nancy that no guest had appeared without a properly marked admission card.

Relieved that not a single suspicious-looking person had been observed in the home, Nancy relaxed a little. Hilda stretched herself comfortably on a lounge.

"We'll have a couple of hours now with nothing to do," she advised Nancy. "Take it easy before the rush starts."

Nancy preferred remaining alert and was standing near the door when a tall man in a striking costume came up and presented a check.

"Madam needs her coat," he said in low tones. "A long, dark-green one. Hurry, please."

Nancy glanced intently at the stranger. She could not see his face plainly, for a white silk scarf that matched his Moorish costume served to mask the lower portion. His intense black eyes disturbed her, however.

She knew the coat he meant without comparing the numbered tickets, for there was no other like it. Deliberately she took her time, pretending she could not find the garment.

"Hurry!" the man urged again, speaking with a slight British accent.

More suspicious than ever, Nancy purposely turned her back and maneuvered to run her hand into the inner pocket of the coat. Instantly her fingers encountered something made of cloth and very soft to the touch.

She quickly took out the object. There was no mistaking what it was.

One of the masks used by the daring members of the Velvet Gang!

CHAPTER XIX

Danger in the Dark

THINKING quickly, Nancy decided not to reveal that she suspected anything.

After tucking the velvet hood back in the pocket, she took the coat from the hanger and handed it over to the man. With a suggestion of a French accent, she inquired:

"Madame is ill? She is leaving the party so soon? Perhaps I can help her?"

"No, thanks," he replied, still keeping his face muffled in the white scarf. "I'll attend to her."

As soon as he was gone, Nancy took off her cap. In its place she substituted the hat she had brought which belonged to Hannah Gruen, and slipped on the housekeeper's loose coat.

"You're in charge here alone," Nancy told the dumfounded Hilda as she darted away. "I doubt if I'll be back."

"Well, I never!" Hilda sputtered. "Leaving me to look after all the coats—"

Unmindful of her protests, Nancy hurried down the hall in pursuit of the man carrying the green coat. Passing the room where Ned was stationed, she gave him a prearranged signal. Immediately he joined her at the stairway.

"What's up?" he demanded. "Have you spotted someone?"

"I think so," Nancy whispered. "Keep an eye on that man in the Moor's costume. No matter what happens, don't let him escape you."

From the staircase, the couple saw him move directly to a bent, white-haired old lady with glasses, who was waiting in the hallway below. She was not costumed.

"You think they're thieves?" Ned whispered.

Nancy did not answer. She watched intently as the man solicitously helped the old lady put on her coat. Then they parted, the man turning toward the dance floor, and the elderly woman moving slowly toward the carriage entrance at the side of the house.

"Follow him, Ned," Nancy said. "I'll watch her."

Ned started off in pursuit. The man dodged in and out among the dancers, and finally headed toward the kitchen.

"Now what could this bird want in the kitchen?" he said to himself.

Even as he wondered, Ned's quarry reached the swinging door to the kitchen, pushed it open, and darted inside.

Now more determined than ever not to lose track of the man, he quickened his pace to a near run. He was just about to dash into the kitchen when a detaining hand fastened on his arm. Ned turned to face one of the caterers.

"Sorry, young man, but you are not supposed to—" the waiter began.

Ned took no time for explanations. He shook himself free and slipped through the door. He found himself in a large pantry and caught sight of the elusive man disappearing through the kitchen to a door that apparently led to the basement.

Heedless of possible danger, Ned hurried across the main kitchen. Reaching the entrance to the cellar, he found it unlocked.

Ned opened the door and peered down the steps, at the same time flipping the basement light switch. Nothing happened. The fugitive must have unscrewed the bulb, Ned thought, in order to delay any pursuers and escape through the basement exit.

Lighting a match, Ned found the handrail and cautiously descended the stairs, looking about him for the fugitive. He was not in sight.

By the time Ned reached the bottom step, the match was burning his fingers and he dropped it.

Velvet Gang and meant to take the silver peacock!

Her pulse racing, Nancy lunged forward to seize the thief. But she snatched only empty air. With amazing agility, the "old lady" side-stepped her. Just then the lights went off throughout the house.

The familiar pattern of operation was being repeated, Nancy thought despairingly. Under protection of total darkness and the resulting confusion, another well-planned robbery was in progress.

Spurred by a realization that the thieves were about to score again, Nancy groped frantically for the "old lady." But suddenly she froze where she stood, as a man's voice behind her commanded:

"Stand where you are! Don't move!"

CHAPTER XX

Captured

NANCY immediately recognized the voice of the man who had given the command to stand still—Detective Ambrose. He had mistaken her for one of the thieves!

Ignoring the order, she kept feeling her way forward and groping for the elusive "old lady." Nancy knew that she could not have moved far away. If only the lights would go on!

"She'll head straight for that silver peacock," Nancy reasoned. "So that's where I'll go."

In the darkness, Nancy stumbled into the table on which it stood. At the same instant she realized the woman was there! Nancy's arms encircled her, and she clung fast.

It seemed to Nancy that she had fastened onto a tigress, so difficult was it to maintain her grasp. The woman wrenched and clawed. But the young detective held on doggedly. When it seemed as if she could not keep her hold another instant, the lights suddenly went on again!

With a gasp of relief, Nancy glimpsed Detective Ambrose down the hall.

"Help me!" she pleaded. "Quick! Before this woman gets away!"

Astonished, the man beheld not only Nancy but her captive. A green-cloaked figure in a black velvet hooded mask.

"She has the peacock!" Nancy cried, as the prisoner vainly tried to hide the long-tailed silver bird beneath her coat.

"Hang on!" Detective Ambrose shouted, bounding forward.

He seized the masked woman and held her firmly while Nancy retrieved the valuable ornament. Then she ripped off the velvet hood. A dark, sullen-looking young woman glared at them defiantly.

Nancy had expected to expose the same Javanese masquerader she had encountered at the Hendricks' party. Instead, she found the smartly dressed traveler who had assisted in George's abduction.

"Trapped, my beauty!" gloated Detective Ambrose. "One less masked thief for the gang to work with! Where are the rest of 'em?"

The woman did not answer him. Instead, she cried out:

"You stupid dick, you can't pin this on me!"

"Old-timer, eh?" he said, referring to the name she used for him.

She ignored his accusation. "Can't you see that this is a frame-up?" she asked. "This girl jammed the mask down over my face just before the lights went on and pushed the peacock under my coat!"

Detective Ambrose merely laughed at the woman's tirade. The accusation was too ridiculous to deserve a reply. He snapped a pair of handcuffs over her wrists.

"Come along, sister," he said.

Meanwhile, Nancy had been digging into the space behind a near-by radiator. On the floor she found the white wig which the masquerader had been wearing.

Before she could tell the detective about it, Mrs. Dwight, accompanied by Mr. Lightner, came hastily down the hall. Both had been fearful of trouble when the lights went out.

"What happened?" Mr. Lightner demanded, while Mrs. Dwight looked as if she were about to faint.

"Well, I guess we got to give Miss Drew credit," the detective said. "She caught the thief!"

"Very fine," said Mr. Lightner. "What I want to know is how this woman got in here."

Detective Ambrose looked a bit sheepish. "We checked all the invitations."

"Did you admit an old lady with white hair?" Nancy questioned.

"Sure," the detective admitted. "But her invitation was properly marked."

Nancy held up the wig. "She was wearing this."

Mrs. Dwight hastened to explain about the invitation to the woman she had never seen.

"It was this way," she said apologetically. "Miss Wilkins, one of the invited guests, called me early this morning to ask if she could bring her elderly aunt and uncle. I told her 'yes,' but explained the necessity for having properly marked invitations."

"You sent the extra ones?" Detective Ambrose demanded.

"Yes, by special messenger to the Hotel Claymore."

"Lady, you never should have done it," the detective said sternly.

"I marked the invitations myself," Mrs. Dwight admitted. "It was a mistake, I realize now, but I know Miss Wilkins well. I had no reason to distrust her."

"This woman ain't nobody's aunt," Detective Ambrose declared. "What's your name, sister?"

"Try to find out!" the prisoner retorted. "You'll learn nothing from me."

Mrs. Dwight at once sought Miss Wilkins among the guests. The young woman immediately denied knowing the prisoner. Further-more, she asserted that she had no aunt nor uncle who had requested invitations.

"Just as I suspected," declared Ambrose. "This woman is a smart cookie. She used Miss Wilkins' name to get a marked invitation."

During the questioning of the prisoner, plain-clothes men had been searching the grounds. Now one of them reported to the detective that none of the gang had been found.

"All the same, this woman wasn't working alone!" Nancy insisted. "A man was with her. He was probably the 'uncle.' I talked to him. Oh, where did he go?"

Suddenly the group was startled by the un-expected appearance in the hallway of a di-sheveled figure. Ned Nickerson! His uniform was torn, his face bruised, and his hair mussed.

"Ned!" Nancy cried in dismay. "You've been in a fight!"

"And how! That fellow you assigned me to follow proved to be tougher than a whole squad of football players."

"He got away?"

"Yes," Ned admitted, disgusted by his failure. "I could have held him, but I had a choice be-tween turning the lights on or letting him go. I thought that by switching them on I might stop a robbery up here."

"And you did," Nancy informed him. "If the

lights hadn't gone on just when they did, I'm sure this woman would have escaped."

Ned told of the fight in the basement. His story was interrupted by Detective Ambrose.

"That's funny! We had a man posted in the basement to watch the lights. What became of him?"

"He wasn't around when I went down there," Ned reported. "I could have used a little help."

Alarmed, Detective Ambrose turned his prisoner over to a plain-clothes man and raced for the basement. Nancy, Ned, Mr. Lightner, and Mrs. Dwight followed him.

The detective entered every cellar room. The missing detective was not in sight and there was no sign of the man who had assailed Ned.

"This is mighty queer," Ambrose muttered. "Mack wouldn't leave his job."

He opened the door of the cold-storage section and uttered a startled exclamation. On the floor, unconscious, lay the missing Mack.

Though apparently the man had not been struck on the head, it took the detective a long while to revive him. Gradually he recovered his senses and said that he had been attacked from the rear. Before he could fight off his assailant he had been drugged. Evidently it was some time before Ned's arrival.

"That's the Velvet Gang's method," Nancy said to Mrs. Dwight.

"It's dreadful! Perfectly dreadful!" the woman said.

While waiting for the police car to arrive, Detective Ambrose again questioned the woman prisoner. "You may as well come clean and tell us how many are in the gang," he urged.

"Gang?" The woman's lips curled insolently. "I'm sure I don't know what you're talking about."

"Your arrest is a mistake, I suppose?"

"It certainly is."

"And your name is Mary Smith?"

"Edith Smith," the woman corrected.

"You're a cool number," Detective Ambrose retorted. "So you're willing to take the rap rather than squeal on the other members of your gang?"

"You'll learn nothing from me," the prisoner replied stubbornly. "So stop wasting words, and let me ride to the station in peace."

After she had been taken away, both Mrs. Dwight and Mr. Lightner complimented Nancy for her quick thinking and prompt action. They also thanked Ned for his part in the affair. Thanks to the efficient work of the young couple, not a single valuable object had been stolen.

"I only wish I'd caught that man," Ned said ruefully.

He and Nancy remained at the party another hour, thoroughly enjoying themselves as guests this time. But the mystery was the chief topic of conversation up to the moment they said good night.

"Well, we've made a start toward clipping the wings of that gang," Ned declared in satisfaction. "Or, I should say, you have. So far I've only been in the background."

"Mighty useful background tonight, Ned!" Nancy smiled, and then became grave. "As for finding the other members of the gang, I wonder."

"What do you mean? You prevented a robbery tonight. You can do it again."

"Maybe. Saturday is the test."

"Why Saturday, Nancy?"

"It's the final date that was marked on the lining of the hooded mask."

"That's so. But after tonight you don't think the Velvet Gang will dare crash another party— at least not right away."

"They'd dare anything, Ned. But what really bothers me is that, so far as I know, no important party is scheduled for that night."

"Then you haven't a single clue as to where something may happen?"

"Not one, Ned. Frankly, I'm worried. I'm afraid that the gang has set Saturday as the day for a big robbery. Oh, if I only knew some way to stop it!"

"Well, here's an idea, Nancy."

CHAPTER XXI

An Important Identification

"You'll make a detective out of me yet, Nancy Drew." Ned laughed, then became serious. "Here's my idea. Who is it that the gang is afraid of?"

"The police, of course."

"That's where you're wrong," Ned said. "It was Nancy Drew they tried to kidnap, not Chief Denny."

Nancy smiled. "Yes. Go on."

"It was you who caught that woman over at the jail. The gang will lie low for a while if you're around. But if you disappear they'll come out of hiding and the police can capture them. Which" —Ned grinned from ear to ear—"will leave you free for the evening—to give me your entire attention."

Nancy laughed. "To think I fell for that! You win, Ned. Only—"

"No *if's* or *but's*. I have tickets for a fraternity picnic and dance some of my local fraternity brothers are giving."

Nancy assured Ned that she wanted to attend the party. "If I should run into a clue, though, that I had to follow up you wouldn't mind, would you?"

"You're a hound for punishment," Ned teased. "Oh, well, if you do get a chance to crack the case, count me in. Another black eye won't matter. And something else. No work Thursday or Friday. Thursday we go to the yacht club races and Fourth of July belongs to your dad, he told me."

"I'll remember."

Early next morning Nancy telephoned the police captain and learned that the prisoner had refused to talk. She suggested bringing Linda Seeley to headquarters to see if she could identify her. It was possible that at some time or other the woman might have called at the Lightner Entertainment Company or attended one of the parties they had arranged.

Hopefully Nancy dressed in a flattering yellow sports dress and picked up Linda at her office. By special permission from the chief of police they were permitted to see the prisoner. Nancy watched closely to see if she would show any sign of recognition of Linda. The girl detective was sure that the woman did, but the sign was so slight that Nancy did not bother to mention it.

"Don't you think it would go easier for you to talk now than to have the police prove you guilty?" Nancy asked the prisoner.

The answer was a hateful glare as the woman turned her back. The girls returned to Chief Denny's office.

"I'm sure I've seen your prisoner before," Linda reported.

"Where?" he asked.

"At the Lightner Entertainment Company. Unless my memory is playing a trick on me, she was in Mr. Lightner's office to see him about a party. She never gave it, though. She seemed more interested in the private collection of Indian and Greek religious masks than she was in having a party."

"Did she talk to Mr. Lightner?" Nancy asked.

"No. To Mr. Tombar. Mr. Lightner was away but Mr. Tombar used his private office. Soon after the woman came in he sent me on an errand."

"So that you couldn't hear their conversation," Nancy remarked.

"I guess so. Nancy, do you think that she's the one who stole those masks?"

"She or someone in the gang."

Chief Denny was very much interested in this bit of information. He suggested that perhaps

Linda could identify something found on the prisoner. Detectives had grilled her several times since her arrest without the slightest success. Not a single clue as to her real identity had been obtained, and every tag had been removed from her clothing.

"But our policewoman did find this," the officer said, taking a piece of unusual jewelry from his desk drawer.

"Oh, yes, that bracelet came from Lightner's," Linda told him. "We rent it to go with a Turkish costume."

"You've been a great help, Miss Seeley," Chief Denny said. "Maybe now that woman will talk."

The girls waited to hear the result, but it was negative. She still would admit nothing.

Nancy was tempted to tell the chief her suspicions about the Blue Iris Inn. But recalling her father's warning that she must have more specific evidence against Tombar before accusing him, she merely said:

"If I should want some police assistance to do a little investigating during the next few days, may I have it?"

"Certainly. Any time, and thanks for your help so far," the officer said.

Nancy drove Linda back to work. On a hunch she asked for Tombar's address and went to the house. As she suspected, it was vacant, and a neighbor told her that he and his wife had moved away rather unexpectedly.

"Do you have his new address?" Nancy asked, thinking to herself that Tombar's sudden departure looked like an admission of guilt.

"No, I don't. They went at night and didn't even say good-by."

"This is my unlucky day," Nancy reflected gloomily.

Her next stop was at Taylor's store where she talked to the young clerk in the receiving and marking department. He assured her that Mr. Snecker was back at work. At the moment, however, he was away from the store, delivering merchandise in one of the trucks.

"I didn't know anyone in your department is supposed to do that," Nancy said.

"We don't as a regular thing," the clerk answered. "But when Mr. Snecker's asthma gets bad, he likes to get out, so he drives sometimes in place of a man who's taking the day off."

Nancy did not comment but she wondered if the manager of Taylor's knew about this.

"Well, will Mr. Snecker be here in the department tomorrow?" she inquired.

"No. He's going to take an extra long Fourth-of-July week end, and is starting on a trip this evening. In fact, he won't even come back after work today."

"Oh, that means he won't return until Monday," said Nancy, greatly disappointed.

Nancy did not want to discontinue work on the case. But with dates of her own and a Fourth-of-July celebration with her father, there was no chance for further sleuthing until Saturday.

But on Saturday morning she discovered that the Taylor Department Store, as well as most businesses in town, was closed. She planned to go to the office of the auctioneer to inquire whether Mr. Tombar had bought any of the furnishings of the Blue Iris Inn. But she found that it would not open until Monday.

"Anyway, I can ride out to the old inn and look around there again," Nancy thought. "I'll be back in plenty of time to dress for the picnic tonight. I wonder if Bess would go along."

Finding a fruit stain on her dress, Nancy changed to another costume. As she was combing her hair, she guiltily realized that she had not visited George for several days.

"I'll stop there on my way," she decided, "then see about Bess."

Bess was there, reading to her cousin. She looked very pretty in a blue tailored dress, but George appeared wan and unhappy.

"My, I'm glad you came, Nancy!" Bess exclaimed. "George has been frightfully worried that something might have happened to you."

"To me! What an idea!" Nancy laughed it off.

"I worry every minute that you'll get into real trouble," George confessed.

"Why, I've been so good lately it hurts," Nancy replied.

She did not explain further, however, not wishing to distress her friend by offering any argument. She could not understand George's strange attitude.

"Where are you going now, Nancy?" Bess asked presently.

"Well, I thought—"

"You're heading somewhere that will lead to danger!" George instantly guessed, and grabbed her friend's arm.

"Now, George, I was only thinking of a little ride into the country to a place called Blue Iris Inn."

"That place! Bess told me about it. At least I got it out of her. You mustn't go there alone, Nancy."

"It only seemed spooky to Bess because the weeds have taken over."

"That's right," Bess said quickly. "I'll go with you, Nancy, if you want to go."

George twisted her hands nervously. "Don't do it," she pleaded. "Anything you girls might learn isn't worth the risk."

Bess and Nancy soothed their chum as best they could.

"Besides," declared Nancy reassuringly, "it'll have to be a short trip. I must be back in a few hours to keep a date with Ned. We're going to a picnic some of his fraternity brothers are giving."

Later, while driving the last mile toward the inn, they began to discuss their friend's bewildering attitude.

"I wish the doctors could find out what's wrong with George," Nancy said.

"What if she never gets better?" Bess wailed.

"Don't suggest such a thing!" Nancy chided. "Now you give me the shivers."

She would have said more had her attention not been drawn to a green automobile some distance ahead. Thinking it best not to overtake it, she deliberately slowed down.

Soon the girls neared the old inn. The car ahead turned into the driveway. Nancy wondered if Tombar was in it.

"Oh, we can't stop there now!" Bess exclaimed in alarm. "We'll be spotted if we do."

Nancy had no intention of stopping. "I'll drive past and park," she told Bess. "We must walk back without being seen so that we can do some sleuthing."

A moment later the girls sighted the car parked near a side entrance of the Blue Iris Inn. As they passed, the driver alighted. Nancy recognized him at once.

"Peter Tombar!" she exclaimed. "If he's here for the reason I think he is, maybe this will turn out to be my luckiest day yet!"

CHAPTER XXII

Prisoners

DRIVING on past the Blue Iris Inn, Nancy pulled up on another side road an eighth of a mile away. She parked the car beside a clump of willows, and the girls tramped back to the deserted building.

"You won't go too close, promise," Bess begged.

"Just close enough to do some looking. We'll find out what Tombar's doing here without his seeing us."

"Okay."

The green sedan still stood on the weed-choked driveway, but Peter Tombar was not in sight.

"He must be inside," Nancy said.

"If he catches us prowling around here, we may run into all that trouble George predicted!" Bess declared uneasily.

"Now don't get jittery," Nancy soothed her. "We'll stay out of sight."

Using the old pines to shield them, the girls circled around to one side of the inn. Nancy crept up cautiously to a boarded window and peered in through a tiny crack.

"You keep watch," she told Bess.

"What do you see?" her friend demanded in an impatient whisper. "Is Tombar in there?"

"Someone's moving around with a flashlight. Yes, it's Tombar all right! But what's become of all the crates and cartons?"

"They're gone?"

"I can't see any, Bess. You remember before they were stacked high."

"You've seen everything you can," Bess whispered, tugging at her friend's hand. "Come on. Let's get away from here."

Nancy held back. In fascination she watched as Peter Tombar lifted a trap door in the floor of the deserted room and disappeared below.

"I can't leave now," Nancy whispered. "Wonder what's in the cellar?"

Bess pulled frantically on her friend's arm.

"Come on, Nancy!" she warned. "A truck is turning in here!"

It was too late for the girls to retreat to the road without being seen. They flattened themselves against the boarded side window, hoping not to be observed.

Luck was with them, for instead of coming all

the way up the drive, the covered truck halted near the road.

As the girls anxiously waited, it backed up again and drove away.

"A Taylor company truck!" Nancy exclaimed. "The store's closed today!"

"The driver saw us!" Bess insisted fearfully.

"Maybe not," Nancy replied. "Anyway, we'll have time to see if Tombar brings up anything from the cellar."

"Let's go now," Bess urged nervously.

Nancy ignored her plea. Peering in through the crack again, she patiently waited.

Soon she saw Mr. Tombar emerge through the trap door. He carried something in his hands.

"Black masks!" Nancy disclosed excitedly.

"Oh, this proves it!" Bess cried. "Tombar is in with the gang!"

"He's probably one of the ringleaders!" Nancy replied. "They're going to use those masks to-night!"

So absorbed did Bess also become in watching the discharged employee of the entertainment company that she forgot her job as lookout. The girls were suddenly awakened to their danger when Tombar started toward the side door of the inn.

"Let's leave, Nancy," Bess urged. "We may be too late to—"

The sentence was never finished. Nancy heard a crackle back of them and turned.

At that instance a hood was thrown over her head by a masked woman who had crept up silently behind her. At the same moment, Bess was seized and her head also covered by a man whose face was concealed by a hood.

Resistance proved useless. Though the girls struggled and tried to free themselves, they were absolutely helpless, for Tombar rushed out to assist his accomplices.

"This is the Drew girl and her friend," the woman reported.

"So!" Tombar exclaimed. "I knew Nancy Drew was spying on me. We'll deal with her presently. Right now, get 'em both out of the way. Harris is coming and I don't want him to catch on."

Nancy and Bess were hustled into the inn and taken down into the dark, musty cellar. There the masks were exchanged for blindfolds, and the girls were bound and gagged.

"You see what happens to people who don't mind their own business?" Tombar taunted them as he ascended the stairs.

Though they could not speak or move, the captives could hear plainly what went on in the rooms above. Presently the real-estate man arrived and was greeted cordially by Peter Tombar.

"I'm glad you drove out today, Mr. Harris," he said courteously. "I've been thinking over your client's offer to buy this place."

"Then you'll sell?"

"If the price is right, and we can make a quick deal. My wife is tired of River Heights. We want to travel. It will have to be an immediate cash sale, though, or it's all off."

"Give me a couple of hours," Mr. Harris was heard to reply. "I think I can swing it."

"Okay. I'll meet you at your office."

Lying on the dusty, damp cellar floor, Nancy unhappily considered her predicament. Mr. Tombar intended to sell the inn and with his cronies leave River Heights before the police caught up with them.

If only she and Bess could escape and bring state troopers there in time to thwart their plan! But their bonds were secure and there was no chance of loosening them.

"And maybe no one will find us," Nancy reflected despairingly as she heard Harris' car leave.

Only George Fayne knew where she and Bess had gone. In the old days, their failure to return to River Heights in a reasonable length of time would have signaled trouble to their friend. But now George was not herself. Could she possibly be depended upon to send help?

Twenty minutes elapsed, then the girls heard

footsteps on the cellar stairs. Their ankles were unbound and the prisoners were pulled rudely to their feet.

"Come along," a man said gruffly. "You're going to be moved."

The girls' hearts sank. Their one chance of rescue was vanishing!

"Unless," Nancy thought, "our rescuers could pick up our trail."

As the girls were prodded up the stairway, Nancy wondered how she might leave a clue. She thought of the buttons on her dress. Could she possibly get one off?

Stumbling sideways against the wall, she deliberately tried to tear one off. Luck favored her. A protruding nail ripped her dress. She heard a button drop on the step!

"It's a slight hope," she thought as her captor yanked her around unceremoniously.

"Keep goin'," he ordered. "No stallin'." When they reached the main floor of the inn, he said, "Okay, Pete."

"Get those girls out of here," Tombar ordered. "And make it snappy. No telling what they have up their sleeves."

The girls' ankles were bound again. Their arms still tied behind them, and with blindfolds and gags in place, they were lifted into a vehicle and laid on the floor. The driver started the motor and pulled out of the driveway at high speed. Nancy and Bess wondered if it was the Taylor truck they had seen backing out of the driveway.

In the front seat were evidently the two who had captured them. The girls were sure that they were speaking in disguised tones.

"If I can catch them off guard," she thought, "maybe they'll speak in their natural voices."

Suddenly Nancy thumped her two feet up and down.

"Florence, what's that?" the man cried.

"That detective up to her tricks again."

Florence Snecker's voice! Was her companion her husband? He did not sound like the man whose voice she had heard in the apartment.

"You girls keep quiet or you'll be sorry," the woman warned. "We don't want no trouble with you!"

Nancy smiled inwardly. She had achieved her purpose, but as to making trouble, what chance did she have? She was bruised from the constant jolting, and her resistance was being lowered momentarily by the long ride. Her head throbbed and her back ached.

She wondered about Bess who had made no move. Was she asleep or had she fainted? When dreadfully frightened, Bess did sometimes black out for a time.

The two girls were at opposite ends of the truck. Nancy tried to reach Bess but the effort was too painful for her to continue. She longed for the journey to end.

Presently the truck slowed down. They must be in a town. After turning several corners, it finally stopped. The motor was switched off, apparently in some back alley, for there were no street noises. Nancy heard the woman remark to her male companion:

"I'm glad our friend's going to Harris instead of waiting for him at the inn. He used good sense to unload on Harris and pull out, too. This town's getting too hot for all of us."

Nancy felt certain that Mrs. Snecker was speaking of Peter Tombar. If so, it meant that he would flee the city as soon as he had collected the cash from the real-estate agent. The police would not find him, even if it occurred to George Fayne to send them to the inn to investigate.

"I wish I'd never been dragged into this deal," Mrs. Snecker whined.

"Oh, shut up," her companion growled. "After tonight, you'll be on easy street."

The girls were hauled out of the truck, untied, and forced to walk into a building. There they were made to sit on the floor while their wrists and ankles were rebound.

"Good-by, blondie," Mrs. Snecker said, giving Nancy a vicious prod with her shoe. "Let's see you run to the police now and tell what you know."

"We'll take you away in a little while to a place where you'll never squeal!" the man added.

A heavy door was rolled shut and locked. The room became silent as a tomb.

Nancy squirmed and twisted but she could not loosen the cords which held her prisoner. Seldom had she been in a more hopeless situation!

She had fully established that Peter Tombar and the Sneckers were working together in the Velvet Gang. Likewise, she was almost certain that they meant to pull one final robbery and flee.

But what good was this knowledge? She was unable to notify the police or even to free herself and Bess. Moreover, these scoundrels meant to take them away and keep them prisoners indefinitely.

"Oh, why did I let myself get caught!" Nancy thought helplessly.

CHAPTER XXIII

A Threat Revealed

In River Heights the long absence of Nancy and Bess had begun to cause alarm.

Hannah Gruen knew something had gone wrong because Nancy had not returned to dress for her date with Ned. The frantic woman had telephoned the Marvin home several times but had always received the same answer. Bess had not telephoned.

At seven o'clock Ned arrived. Hearing that Nancy had not come home, he said:

"I was afraid of this. She becomes so completely wrapped up in a mystery. Now something's happened." He began pacing the floor.

"Mr. Drew won't be home until late," Hannah informed him. "I've tried to reach him by telephone but I can't. I don't know what to do about Nancy and Bess."

Tearfully she disclosed that the two girls had been seen last at the Marvin home. At that time they had told George that they might drive out to a place called the Blue Iris Inn.

"But nobody seems to know where it is. The inn's not listed in the phone book."

"I never heard of the place until Nancy mentioned it," Ned admitted. "And she didn't say where it was."

"Oh, Ned, can't you think of something we can do?" the housekeeper pleaded.

"I'll go out to the inn as soon as I find out where it is," the young man promised. "Maybe George can give me a clue."

Leaping into his car, he drove to the Fayne home. George was up and dressed, but in a near state of collapse from worry after talking with her mother and Mrs. Marvin about the girls' disappearance.

"Oh, I was afraid this would happen!" George moaned. "I warned Bess and Nancy not to go, but they wouldn't listen to me. Now the dreadful threat may be carried out."

"Threat?" Ned demanded. "What threat, George?"

"I don't dare tell you."

"You must! Nancy and Bess may be in serious trouble. That's the only way to help them."

"If I tell you, we may all be harmed."

Ned whistled. "Is it that bad?" he asked.

"Now listen, George, this may be a life-and-death matter."

"That's right," her mother said. "Don't let your fears mean more to you than Nancy and Bess's safety."

The words stunned George and suddenly brought a marked change in her attitude. The old fire came back into her eyes and the color returned to her cheeks.

"Of course I'll help find Nancy and Bess," she said with determination. "I don't know what ailed me. Instead of helping Nancy, I've really been hindering her by not telling what I know."

"Tell us quickly!" Mrs. Marvin urged.

"Well," George began, "after those kidnapers drugged me I seemed to lose my nerve. That woman's words just burned into my brain. She warned me that if I didn't make Nancy drop the case great harm would come not only to her but to Mrs. Gruen and Mr. Drew and my family and Bess's."

"Oh, George, you should have reported this to the police," Mrs. Fayne cried.

"I didn't dare. But now I don't care. We must find Nancy and Bess."

"What else did the kidnapers say?" Ned asked. "It might be a clue to what happened to Nancy and Bess."

"Well, at the end of the threats, the woman said, 'We'll put Nancy on ice in the flour cellar!'

I've wondered ever since what they meant by that."

"A flour cellar?" Mrs. Marvin murmured. "What significance would that have?"

"I never heard of a flour mill around here," Ned said thoughtfully. "George, maybe they meant f-l-o-w-e-r cellar."

"That might have been it," she agreed. "Do you suppose there's one in the Blue Iris Inn? Wait! Nancy told me about a real-estate agent who has been wanting to buy that place for someone. I'll ask him."

Excitedly, and now apparently completely recovered, George flew to the telephone and called Mr. Harris. When she rejoined the group in the living room, her face was worried but determined.

"I've learned a lot," she said. "Mr. Harris told me the inn once had a small greenhouse specializing in blue iris. The cellar of the inn was used for sorting bulbs and arranging cut flowers."

"Nancy and Bess are probably prisoners in the cellar there!" Ned cried. "But where is it?"

"Mr. Harris gave me directions," George replied. "And listen to this. He also told me that he had arranged today to buy the inn from Mr. Tombar for a client."

"Tombar! Nancy suspected him all along," Ned cried.

"Mr. Harris was supposed to have delivered the money to him at his office, but he had trouble raising it on such short notice, so he told Tombar to come back Monday."

"Maybe Tombar went back to the inn!" Ned exclaimed. "If he did, we can catch him and find out about the girls!"

"I'm going too," George announced with spirit. "No, don't try to stop me, anyone! Nancy and Bess are in danger, and I want to help."

The rescue party, Ned, Mr. Marvin, George, and her father, assembled quickly. As they were ready to drive off, Mrs. Gruen telephoned that she finally had reached Mr. Drew.

"He has notified the state police and is on his way to the inn himself right now," she said. "Oh, get there as fast as you can!"

Reaching the Blue Iris Inn some time later, Ned's party learned from the state troopers that Nancy's parked car already had been found. They had broken into the boarded-up building and searched thoroughly. But they had found no trace of the missing girls or of their abductors.

"The question is, were the girls ever here?" Mr. Drew said. "There's nothing to prove it."

"Let me look," George said, borrowing a flash-light from one of the policemen.

It was not until she came to the cellar of the inn that George found a clue. There was evidence that a scuffle had taken place. She pointed out that some of the footprints had been made by the type of shoes Nancy and Bess wore. They were also on the stairway.

"And look at this!" George exclaimed gleefully, picking up the button Nancy had dropped. "This was on the dress Nancy was wearing!"

"You're sure?" a policeman asked.

"I'm positive."

"Now we have something to work on," the officer said excitedly. "No doubt the girls were taken away from here in the car or the truck. We'll try to follow them."

By inspecting the tire marks the police figured out that the truck and the car, both in arriving and leaving the inn, had taken a direction toward River Heights.

"That proves the kidnapers are the same gang Nancy has been trying to catch," Ned declared.

"Not exactly," a trooper spoke up. "And if they did go as far as where heavy traffic begins, it'll be almost impossible to follow the tracks."

Mr. Drew gloomily agreed. "The best thing to do is broadcast a general alarm for Mr. Tombar's green car," he declared. "You may be able to stop it somewhere."

"We'll do everything we can," the officer promised. "But the girls may be in the truck and we have no description of that. And don't forget, those bandits have a big start too. They may be a hundred miles from here by now."

"On the other hand, they may be only a few miles away," Ned cut in. "Nancy had a strong hunch that the Velvet Gang planned to pull a last big job tonight. If she's right, they won't leave town until they have the loot."

"Her idea is a good one," the officer conceded. "It won't help us rescue her and Miss Marvin, though. By the time we get a report on the robbery, the gang will be on their way to another place."

"And taking Nancy and Bess with them!" George cried.

"All the more reason why we must set up road blocks," Mr. Drew urged. "We've delayed too long now."

As he started for his car, the lawyer noticed that Ned had remained behind. He turned and waited for him to catch up.

"Hurry, Ned!" he called to him, as the young man stood looking up at the building. "We've got to make it snappy."

The young man shook his head. "I'm staying here."

"Staying?"

"Yes. I've decided to remain and guard this place, Mr. Drew. Maybe I'm crazy, but there's an outside chance that the gang may come back here tonight."

"But we're trying to save the girls."

"They may bring Nancy and Bess with them."

"You're going to stay alone?" Mr. Drew said dubiously. "How about one of the police—"

"I'll be okay," Ned insisted. "We can't afford to tie down a police officer just on the slim chance that I'm right. Maybe no one but Tombar will show up."

"But he may carry a pistol, Ned," Mr. Drew pointed out. "It seems to me you're taking an awful chance. Better come along with us."

"I'll watch my step. I've got two good fists," the athlete said grimly, "and I'm used to tackling opponents on short notice.

"What's more, if I ever meet that fellow who nailed me in the basement of the Dwight house, I want to pay him back!"

CHAPTER XXIV

Fire!

LEFT together in their dark prison room, Bess and Nancy were suffering intense discomfort. Their gags made breathing difficult, and the cords cut deeply into their flesh.

"Those men made a thorough job of seeing that we don't get away," Nancy thought ruefully.

So tightly had her wrist bonds been tied that she realized that she could never unfasten them without aid. The ropes about her ankles were somewhat looser, but it was impossible to reach them.

"I'll wiggle around and perhaps I'll find something to help me," Nancy thought hopefully. "And where is Bess?"

As she rolled and twisted on the floor, Nancy brushed against an object with a sharp metal edge. It seemed to be a loose strap around a large box.

At once Nancy took hope. Raising her bound feet, she began to saw the cords up and down across the metal. It was the hardest kind of work. Repeatedly she abandoned the task as fatigue overcame her. But after each rest period she would try again.

Finally success was hers! The frayed ankle cords broke. Her feet were free!

Nancy scrambled up, and though she still could not see because of the blindfold, she groped backward with her tied hands until she found the sharp piece of metal. Another five minutes and both hands were free.

"What a relief!" she gasped, jerking off the blindfold and removing the gag.

Her unlighted prison was apparently window-less. Nancy was conscious of piles of crates and boxes all about her. Where was she?

Not knowing whether there was a guard near by, she did not dare call out Bess's name. She would just have to find her by stumbling around.

As she started her search, Nancy's head en-countered an overhead, swinging light bulb. She switched it on.

The brightness revealed that she and Bess had been left captives in a shipping room. Nancy wondered if it was Taylor's Department Store.

After a hunt in the aisles between the crates, she found Bess.

Quickly Nancy freed her friend and pulled her

to her feet. Bess found it difficult to walk because her arms and legs had become numb.

"Oh, Nancy!" she cried out.

"Sh! Someone may be listening," Nancy warned.

"Where are we?" Bess asked in a whisper, her voice quavering with fright.

"In the receiving and shipping room of Taylor's store, I think."

"Let's get out," Bess urged.

She hobbled to a heavy metal door at the far end of the room. It was locked!

"I was afraid of it," Nancy muttered. "Now—"

She suddenly switched off the light, aware of voices on the other side of the heavy door.

Nancy tiptoed over and the girls pressed their ears against it and listened.

A man was talking, bragging about the ease with which the two girls had been captured. He reported that they were neatly tied up and ready for their second ride in another half hour.

"If we hadn't caught that Drew girl she might have interfered with us tonight. And nobody's goin' to stop me from takin' a big haul out of old man Taylor's store!" his voice came to them. "Once we get the silver and the furs, we'll pick up those girls and beat it. And you," he said to someone, "come back here in ten minutes to be sure everything's okay."

Nancy's pulse began to pound. So the Velvet

Gang was going to rob Taylor's Department Store! She must stop them! But how?

"Let's scream for help," Bess whispered.

"No, Bess! That would only bring them in here to tie us up again. Maybe there's a telephone in here."

The girls waited until they thought their captors had left, then turned on the light. Though they found a desk, there was no telephone on it.

"Now what'll we do?" Bess asked.

"You examine the walls for any kind of exit," Nancy suggested. "There may be a hole of some kind to shove boxes through. I want to find out what these boxes contain."

"Just Taylor Department Store goods probably."

"Maybe, but I have another idea. This big cardboard carton looks exactly like one I saw at the Blue Iris Inn!"

"How would it get here?"

"Snecker uses a Taylor truck, don't forget. Furthermore, he's in charge of this room."

"But why would he bring the cartons here, Nancy? It doesn't make sense."

Without attempting to answer, Nancy tore open the top of the carton. The first item she lifted out was the Indian religious mask which had been stolen from Mr. Lightner.

"Here's proof!" she whispered excitedly.

As Bess examined the walls for a means of

escape, Nancy went on with her task.   Under-
neath some shredded tissue she found other masks
which she knew had been taken from the entertainment firm.

Nancy moved on to another carton.   In it she
found the silver miniatures which had been
snatched from Gloria Hendrick's home!

"I've found the loot!" Nancy excitedly told
Bess who had now reached the third wall without
locating a door or chute.

"Wonderful!   But that doesn't get us out of
here."

Bess examined the fourth wall.   No better luck.
Nancy had opened two more cartons.   Both contained stolen goods.

"But these boxes are all marked with the Taylor
store name!" Bess said.

"To fool the police, Bess.   The thieves packed
the stolen goods in them at the inn.   Then Snecker
or some of his helpers would bring them here.
Snecker marked the cartons as damaged merchandise to be returned to the original shipper."

"The shippers are in the gang?"

"No.   They're innocent.   The boxes never
reached them.   You will notice there are only two
factories.   One of the gang must work in each
factory which is in a distant city.   He takes the
loot out and delivers it to a pawnbroker or some
other fence."

"All of these boxes and crates are being shipped by the thieves?" Bess gasped.

"Oh, no, they couldn't get by with that. Most of the boxes are incoming merchandise. See, here's one marked *Sweaters*."

"And here's another stamped *China*," Bess added. "That big one is filled with toys."

Nancy had made the same observation. Curious to learn if the box actually contained toys, she ripped open the top.

"Toys all right," she conceded. "Games, an atom bomb set, a chemical set and—say! This gives me an idea!"

"What?" Bess demanded eagerly.

"Maybe we'll get out of here yet!"

"Oh, I hope so. But how, Nancy?"

"This chemical set! See, this one package is marked *smoke!* By mixing the chemicals, we can make it appear that there is a fire here when one of them returns."

"And maybe start a real one!"

"No danger of that, Bess. Listen at the door while I whip up a 'fire.' Maybe someone's out there now."

Bess pressed her ear against the steel door. She could hear a hum of voices. Then a man said, "It won't be long now. I'll be back in twenty minutes."

Bess now could hear only one person moving

around in the next room. She conveyed the information to Nancy.

"Good! My smoke preparation is ready. Now we'll see if it works. Get some rope and turn out the light."

Bess snatched up the cords, gag, and blindfold which had been used on her and then snapped off the swinging overhead bulb.

Crouching down on the floor by the locked door, Nancy began to blow smoke from the chemical set beneath the crack.

"We might yell 'fire,' " Bess whispered, hopeful of quick action.

"That would reveal we've taken off our gags, Bess. I want to surprise the guard."

Patiently Nancy kept blowing smoke under the door crack. Suddenly she was rewarded. From the other side of the door, the girls heard a startled exclamation.

"He's noticed the smoke!" Nancy murmured to Bess. "Stand back!"

Scarcely had the two girls flattened themselves against the wall than the metal door was unbolted and pushed back.

As the guard rushed in, looking about in bewilderment and sniffing the smoke-laden air, Nancy extended her foot directly in his path.

Down he went, sprawling in an ungainly heap on the floor!

CHAPTER XXV

Unmasked

IN A flash, Nancy and Bess seized the man's arms and legs and held him down. He kicked and fought but could not get away.

"Quick! Help me tie him up!" Nancy directed her friend.

Efficiently they bound the man's hands and ankles and stuffed the gag in his mouth. Nancy switched on the light for a moment to look at the captive.

"I'm sure he was one of George's kidnapers!" she exclaimed. "Are you Mr. Snecker?" she asked him.

He remained motionless, glaring at her malignantly.

She must find out! Slipping her hand into his coat pocket, she pulled out a wallet. Opening it, Nancy found a driver's license issued to Burt Snecker.

"Maybe he has a key to the store!" Nancy thought.

The clerk's keys were handy. Under the circumstances Nancy thought it permissible to borrow them and get into the store.

"We must prevent the robbery if we can, Bess," she said. "Come on!"

The girls closed the heavy metal door behind them and tiptoed through an adjoining darkened room. Crossing the alley between the buildings, Nancy tried one key after another in the first door she came to. At last she found one that fit. She turned it and quietly let herself and Bess in.

"Do be careful," her friend urged. "Nancy, there ought to be a night watchman around. Where is he?"

"I wish I knew."

The girls ascended a short pair of stairs and pushed a swinging door which opened into the first floor of the store.

"Ghosts!" whispered Bess as she stared at the white-draped sales counters and merchandise.

She and Nancy moved forward in the dimly lighted building until the jewelry counter came to view. Two women and a man who wore velvet masks were systematically looting the glass cases of their valuable pieces!

"How dreadful!" Bess murmured. "What'll we do? We can't capture all three."

"With luck, we can," Nancy whispered. "We'll find a phone and call the police."

Quietly retreating, the girls located a telephone booth in the rear. Nancy called headquarters. She had hardly spoken her name when Chief Denny said:

"Where are you? There's a three-state alarm out for you!"

"In Taylor's. There's a robbery going on. Come quick! I'll meet you at the employees' entrance in the alley."

"We'll be right there!"

The girls crept back to see what was happening in the jewelry department. Time seemed to drag.

"I wish the police would hurry," Bess whispered uneasily. "If they don't get here soon—"

Just then the girls heard the wail of a police siren from the street. The sound also reached the ears of the masked thieves.

"The cops!" exclaimed one of the women shrilly. "We've got to get out o' here!"

In panic the three rushed for the employees' entrance. But Nancy and Bess had hurried there ahead of them and blocked their way.

Seeing that escape was cut off, the man wheeled and ran in the opposite direction. The women made the mistake of trying to overpower Nancy and Bess.

They were still engaged in a fierce struggle

when the police, led by Detective Ambrose, rushed up with clubs. Both women were seized and handcuffed.

"The man with them got away!" Nancy gasped. "But another, Burt Snecker, is tied up in the shipping room."

Two officers started a search while another removed the masks from the two women.

"Florence Snecker!" Nancy cried, recognizing one of them.

The other was the woman who had costumed herself as a Javanese beauty and had otherwise disguised her appearance. Both glared at Nancy with hate in their eyes.

Though the police searched the store from roof to cellar, the only person they found was the night watchman bound and gagged in the elevator. Snecker was brought from the shipping room, and the three prisoners were taken to the office of Mr. Taylor, who had been summoned by Ambrose and had just arrived.

No accurate check or inventory was possible, since the missing thief had taken a quantity of jewelry, but Mr. Taylor estimated that Nancy and Bess had saved the store a huge loss.

"I can't thank you enough, Miss Drew. How did you ever trail these people?"

Nancy gave a brief account of the case, ending with, "I began to suspect Snecker when I found out that he was a friend of Mr. Tombar's. I wonder if the man who escaped could be Tombar."

"Is he?" Ambrose asked his prisoners.

Silence.

"I'll make you talk!" the detective barked.

Assisted by Nancy, who supplied much of the evidence, he rigidly questioned the three. At first they refused to talk, but after he warned them that their sentences would be lighter if they confessed, Mrs. Snecker finally broke down. She gave a whining account of her part in the sordid affair, which was mostly writing letters to a certain pawnshop dealer and another fence. This was her first burglary job, she insisted.

"If we're going to jail, so are the others!" Snecker burst out bitterly. "There are two men in this who are more guilty than we are."

"Tell your story," Detective Ambrose said. "First of all, what's the right name of that woman we're holding in jail?"

"Mrs. Ridley. She's Mrs. Snecker's half sister," the man answered sullenly. "She didn't join the gang until lately."

"And your name?" the detective demanded.

"She's Ermintrude Schiff, an actress," Snecker informed him as the woman remained stubbornly silent. "If she hadn't been hard up for cash, she wouldn't have been mixed up in it, either."

Snecker then went on to place most of the blame on Peter Tombar, who, he said, had worked closely with Mrs. Snecker's brother, the man who had escaped from the store.

"What's his name?" Ambrose asked, jotting down the information Snecker had provided.

"Jerry Goff. He's well educated, Jerry is. He uses an Oxford accent sometimes to impress people."

"And also to disguise his voice," Nancy thought, recalling her adventure of being almost suffocated at one of the parties. Aloud she said, "Wasn't he the man who wore the black cloak at the Hendricks' masquerade?"

"Yes. Tombar lent it to him. When you found a hole in it, Tombar took the cloak away in a hurry."

"This Jerry Goff was one of the men who helped with George Fayne's abduction, wasn't he?" Nancy asked.

"Yes. He sat in front of you."

"You were in on it, too, weren't you?" Nancy prodded.

"Yes," Snecker admitted. "I helped Mrs. Schiff. We muffed the job getting the wrong girl." He said that Tombar's wife was not involved in any way.

"You also slipped up when you dropped your department-store charge plate."

"It fell out of my breast pocket when I leaned out the car window. It wouldn't have mattered except that Miss Drew found out."

"Then you must have been the one who advised the store employees not to turn in their plates after the credit manager gave the order," Nancy remarked.

"Sure," Snecker said with a shrug. "I sent around a fake order. I knew I'd be caught if all the plates except mine came in."

Questioned further, Snecker identified Jerry Goff as the member of the gang who made friends with the servants and kitchen help at various parties. In this way he could slip unchallenged to the basement and switch off the lights.

"Jerry thought up the scheme in the first place and sold Tombar the idea," Snecker disclosed. "But if it hadn't been for Tombar, the rest of us never would've got in this mess."

"He planned all the robberies?" Nancy questioned.

"Every one. He gave us a list of the places we were to knock off, supplied masks and costumes, and room plans of the houses."

"And cards to admit you?"

"Oh, sure. Tombar thought of everything. Or he did until you made the going tough, Miss Drew. Then he began to make stupid mistakes."

"Tell me how the stolen Marie Antoinette miniature got to the store's gift department," Nancy asked.

"It was a slip-up. The miniatures were at Tombar's hide-out in the country. By mistake I put that one in my pocket and my helper saw it. I had to send it to the gift department then, and I didn't dare recall it. In my excitement I marked it at a ridiculously low price."

Nancy next asked Snecker if he had any idea how Peter Tombar might be captured.

"He'll get out of town as quick as he can," the clerk replied. "But he may have headed back to the country to get some things he had stored in the inn."

With this full confession, the three prisoners were escorted to headquarters to be booked on robbery and kidnaping charges. Bess and Nancy accompanied the officers to make a report on their part in the capture. While they were talking to Chief Denny, Mr. Drew hurried in with George, her father, and Mr. Marvin.

"Nancy! Bess!" George cried wildly, flinging her arms about them. "You're safe!"

Mr. Drew clasped his daughter in his arms, and Mr. Marvin hugged Bess. Information was exchanged hurriedly. Nancy was thrilled at the change in George and whispered this to Bess.

"Yes, isn't it wonderful!" she answered.

When Nancy learned a few minutes later that Ned had remained at the Blue Iris Inn as guard in case one of the abductors should return, she became alarmed.

"We think Peter Tombar may go back there, especially if Goff gets word to him what happened in the store," Nancy told her father. "If Ned should be taken by surprise—"

"We'll return there right now," Mr. Drew broke in. "And we'd better notify the state police to meet us there."

"I hope we're not too late," Nancy said as they raced from the station house.

George insisted upon going along, despite protests from Bess and Mr. Fayne.

"I feel fine," she insisted stubbornly. "Now that I know the Velvet Gang is nearly rounded up my worries are ended. I guess it was the threat more than anything else that kept me down. This excitement tonight has cured me!"

"Ah, that's our old George," Mr. Fayne declared happily. "It seems like old times to hear you talk that way."

At the Blue Iris Inn two troopers were waiting for them. Neither Ned nor the escaped leader of the party thieves was in evidence. Finding the rear door unlocked, they rushed in. A muffled shout reached them from the kitchen area.

"Come here!" Ned called. "I need help!"

Everyone rushed to the kitchen. The officers' flashlights disclosed Peter Tombar pinned to the floor, with Ned sitting on his midriff.

"I'm sure glad you got here," the youth said in obvious relief. "I've been holding this guy for half an hour, trying to figure out a way to get him to headquarters."

Relieved of his prisoner, Ned related how he had broken in and hidden in the old inn. His wait had not been in vain. Tombar had arrived by taxi.

"I think he has a car in one of the buildings here," Ned disclosed. "Likewise, a lot of money in the cupboard under the sink. He was just reaching for the roll when I tackled him."

Tombar's clothing had been torn in the fight and both eyes were blackened. Glaring at Nancy from beneath swollen lids, he savagely berated her for the capture of the Velvet Gang. Still fuming, he was taken off by the troopers.

Later that night Goff was caught as he attempted to board a plane at the River Heights airport. Several days elapsed before Nancy and her friends were assured that the two remaining members of the band had been rounded up. The police arrested a pawnbroker in one city and a fence in another.

Dozens of cartons of silver and other valuables stolen from River Heights homes were recovered and returned to their owners. In a few instances, missing treasures already sold could not be traced. The owners were promised that the money recovered at the Blue Iris Inn would nearly repay them for their losses.

Mr. Lightner's valuable ceremonial masks which Nancy had found in the shipping room of

Taylor's store were returned. He came to call personally one evening to thank her.

"I value these masks almost as much as I do my business," he told the girl and her father. "And you saved both for me."

"By the way, Mr. Lightner," interposed Carson Drew, "I have good news for you. Your troubles are really at an end. We'll have no damage suits to defend. Your clients have agreed to settle for the amounts you offered to make up the small differences."

"All the claims against me will be dropped, and there'll be no notoriety?"

"Yes. Your customers are happy to have recovered most of their heirlooms. I have the signed releases in my pocket."

"That's wonderful! Wonderful!" Mr. Lightner declared. "Again I say, I owe everything to Nancy. Don't you agree, Mr. Drew?"

"If I weren't afraid of turning her pretty head with too much praise, I might really air an opinion!" The lawyer laughed.

At this moment Bess, George, and Ned arrived. After Mr. Lightner had been introduced to them, he told the trio why he was there at the Drews'.

"There's so little I can do to show my appreciation," he added. "But I'm giving Nancy a mask as a small token of my gratitude."

"Not a velvet hooded mask?" Nancy joked.

"No, indeed. We're through with those forever. I'm giving you an ancient mask of a beautiful Egyptian queen."

The man smiled and from a box took two identical masks. It was evident that one was very old, the other a new copy.

"How lovely!" Nancy exclaimed. "Thank you very much, Mr. Lightner. But why two of them?"

"One for your own museum, one to wear to a masquerade."

"That may not be for some time," Nancy said.

"It's sooner than you think," Ned spoke up, grinning. "We had to miss the picnic last Saturday, so the fellows decided on another summer party—this time a masquerade. You'll go as an Egyptian queen."

"What fun!"

"Nancy ought to go as the Queen of Mystery," Bess remarked. "It won't be long before she'll be in the midst of another puzzle."

Bess's prophecy came true when Nancy was confronted with one of the most puzzling problems of her sleuthing career and had to ask her friends to help her solve *The Ringmaster's Secret*.

"What are you girls going to wear to the masquerade?" she questioned Bess and George.

"You know me—always Bopeep." Bess giggled.

"I'll have to think it over," George replied.

"But there's one person I know I'll never try to imitate."

"Who is she?" Bess asked.

"That well-known detective Nancy Drew." George pretended to shiver. "I tried it once and found it too dangerous!"